IN THE EMPIRE OF THE
GOLDEN DRAGON

IN THE EMPIRE OF THE
GOLDEN DRAGON

BEN RAHA

authorHOUSE®

AuthorHouse™
1663 Liberty Drive
Bloomington, IN 47403
www.authorhouse.com
Phone: 1-800-839-8640

First published by AuthorHouse   11/21/2011

ISBN: 978-1-4670-8167-2 (sc)
ISBN: 978-1-4670-8168-9 (hc)
ISBN: 978-1-4670-8169-6 (ebk)

Library of Congress Control Number: 2011919904

Printed in the United States of America

Ben Raha was born at Kiev, Ukraine, on June 21, 1998. Three month later his family emigrated to Pennsylvania USA. From a young age, Ben was interested in books, from where he could get answers to all his unlimited questions. At the age of 5 his grandmother Anna, a professional teacher, taught him how to read and write. Being a bilingual and having a great hunger for knowledge Ben started "comiendo libros", devouring book by book. But the real story began at age 12 when Ben Raha started writing his own book. Now young readers can enjoy his first book, "In the Empire of the Golden Dragon". His second book "Orphan Alex, the son of Soviets" is dedicated to his grandfather Aleksey. What Ben has learned himself, he also shares with others; courage, good work, and perseverance *will* eventually pay off.

龙1 AT HOME

"Hello, Mr. Harper! I'm glad you came! Oh, Mr. and Mrs. Smith!" said Mr. Wang. He bowed nearly to the ground before a richly dressed couple as they came in. "Oh, Mrs. Rouges, how do you do? And you, Arthur, old friend, what a spiffy suit you have! And your children look so nice!" he said as two young girls entered, holding stiff parasols. The guests took off their snow-covered cloaks and stepped into the parlor of the house. The ladies went into the living room to sip tea with Mrs. Wang, while the men went into the den to discuss politics and stock market prices. As more guests came in, the house got noisier, but the adults seemed not to notice.

The children ran around the house playing hide-and-seek. "Ninety-eight, ninety-nine, one hundred! Ready or not, here I come!" shouted Jake, bursting out of the closet. Their maid, Mrs. Tobin, almost had a heart attack when she saw the dirty boy run right by her. Jake raced to the grand staircase and started to climb. He spied a figure sitting on a chandelier high above him. "Lucy! I see you!" he yelled. He ran into the empty guest room, which concealed a thousand and one hiding places. He thought he saw the pillows move, and when he yanked them off, there was one of the Bradford twins, giggling. He opened the wardrobe and went inside to look through the clothes. Checking the back corner, he heard the wardrobe door slam. When he opened it, a stampede of children rushed out. He raced into the hallway, but too late. Suddenly he saw one of the potted plants move.

He crept over to it and found three boys hiding in the branches. He looked around and moved off down the hallway.

All the guests had arrived, when suddenly there came a sharp knock on the door. Mr. Wang opened the door, and there stood his twin brother, Mr. Fung. Mr. Fung was a tall man with black hair. His face was long and thin, with piercing, ice-blue eyes; a long, crooked nose; and high cheekbones. In his right hand he carried a cobra skin walking stick topped by the snake's head. The eyes glowed green, with flashes of red in them. The mouth was open, seemingly ready to strike. The gleaming fangs curved downward in an arc. Rattlesnake rattles hung at the end of the stick, with a sharp point sticking out. Around his waist hung a sharp, curving sword; three daggers were hidden among his silk clothes. His ruffled pants were covered with a long black skirt. Over his black shirt with silver and ruby dragon emblems, he wore a vest covered with lizard scales. Around his neck hung a diamond dragon brooch with ruby eyes and emerald claws. A silk turban set with pearls was on his head. As Mr. Fung took off his black cloak, he revealed a small sack of gold coins at his waist. A modern iPhone was in his breast pocket.

He bowed deeply and strode into the den. His son Suo followed, carrying a small sword at his waist. Mr. Fung turned around and said, "Suo, go enjoy yourself! Play with the other children! Your toys are in your backpack." The children and even some of the adults laughed. Imagine, a fourteen-year-old boy bringing toys to a friend's house! Suo turned red and rushed upstairs. He turned the corner at the top of the staircase and raced down a dark hallway. Suddenly he heard someone. It was Sally, trying to hide. Suo hid behind a pot of geraniums and waited until Sally went by. Then he opened his backpack and pulled out a screwdriver, a laser, a flashlight, a box of various tools, and a switch machine he had invented that sent two hundred volts of electricity into anything the little wire touched. He planned to open any locked safes with it. Then he took out a hamburger and started munching.

Downstairs Mr. Fung was listening to the men's debates with scorn. "But, Mr. Smith, I *insist* that the stock market has risen six percent since last night, and not five and a half!" Mr. Harding exploded "That would mean that if I invested in the Cauldron deal, I would gain two hundred and fifty thousand. But my broker claims sales will pitch downward twelve percent, which would mean my company would be affected, causing me to lose four million, three-hundred seventy-three thousand, four-hundred and eighty-one dollars and fifteen cents!" he said, his eyes bulging at the very thought. Mr. Fung snickered and yawned when Mr. Harding proceeded with his lecture. "That would be a tremendous loss for my company and would shut down our chances of signing that deal with that apple sauce company! Or was it some sort of computer store?" he muttered. Mr. Fung held his iPhone and tapped at the apple symbol. "I think you might mean Apple industries?" he inquired with a smirk.

Mr. Smith couldn't contain himself any longer and burst out, "But I said that the stocks *dropped* five and a half percent! Not rose! That m-means that I have made a bad deal with Worldwide Electro! Now my company will lose not four, but *forty*, million dollars! This shall be my ruin!" he shrieked.

"Relax, Mr. Smith! You still have several hundred million left!" cackled Mr. Fung. Mr Smith's jaw dropped down and as the comical situation settled in, he fainted dead away. Finally Mr. Fung tired of making a sport on the businessmen's talking and asked, "Where is your restroom lo-cated?" with a slight Chinese accent.

"Top floor, down the hallway. It'll be on your left!" said Mr. Wang as he sprayed smelling salts on Mr. Smith's face. Mr. Fung bowed and exited the room.

As soon as the door behind him was safely shut, Mr. Fung grinned. "Brainless fools! To think that we're actually related!" He chuckled. He crept up the banister and ran into the dark hallway. Jake was just ahead of him, but Mr. Fung did not see him in the dark. But Jake heard him, and he quickly hurried into the huge starlight room, which had a dome. He spotted Sally. "Get down here and be quiet!" he hissed. Sally looked puzzled but came down. The teens hid behind a large couch and watched as their cousin Suo and uncle Fung met.

Mr. Fung grabbed Suo roughly and dragged him to the door of their father's office. The kids watched as Mr. Fung took out a glowing key, made entirely from the backbone of a cobra. The key gleamed light blue in the darkness. As Mr. Fung inserted it into the elaborate keyhole, it shone brighter and brighter. Then a sharp *click* sounded, ands the key instantly stopped glowing. The job was completed. The door to their father's personal office opened. Sally and her brother gasped! No one except their father was allowed in his office. Even they, his children had been in it only seven times. Jake jumped up and raced to the open door. He peeked in and saw Suo place a weird contraption on Mr. Wang's desk. He stuck a little wire into the keyhole and pressed a red button. Jake laughed silently, confident the electronic fingerprint and password system and the computer-protected camera and voice recognition security would thwart Suo.

Suddenly there was a buzzing noise, and the desk shook violently. With a groan it cracked in two. Sally shook with rage. How dare these worthless relatives destroy their property! Sally shot into the room and sent Mr. Fung out the window with a kung fu kick. Mr. Fung didn't even have time to yell before the cold waters of the pond below closed over his head. Quickly Jake grabbed Suo and swung him against a replica of an ancient samurai warrior. Suo hit the sheathed blade and groaned. But Jake was not finished yet. He flipped Suo onto the cracked desk and grabbed the remote. "Let's see how you'll dance with two hundred volts of electricity running through your veins," he laughed and pressed the button. Suo flipped into the air, blue lightning bolts shooting from his fingertips. Jake grinned and pressed a lever. *Kablam!* The device exploded, sending Suo out the window. Just as Mr. Fung resurfaced, his son crashed into the pond.

As Jake and Sally raced outside, Suo climbed onto what looked like a little island. Jake waved his hand over the motion sensor, and the little island Suo was sitting on came alive and sent Suo screaming into the air. He splashed back into the pond and pushed away a sinking "rock." The "rock" grew a head and bit Suo's rear end. "Waaaaah!" he cried as two curious trout tugged off his shoes. A largemouth bass grabbed the shiny buckle and undid Suo's belt. Off came his pants.

Meanwhile Mr. Fung was having troubles of his own. First of all, his shoes got stuck in the seaweed. His sword went down next, and just as he was sure he was in the worst position possible, a large fish grabbed his brooch and made off with it. Mr. Fung dogpaddled to shore and crawled up the bank. "Aaaaaaaugh!" screamed some cute chicks as he came out. "A mud monster! Help us!" they screamed and promptly fainted. Just as they came to, out of the water stumbled Suo, searching for his pants. He saw the girls staring at him. His face turned crimson, and he tried to hide his whites behind a lily pad. The girls started to giggle. Only then did Suo become aware of the frog and the lily pad, which were residing on his head. Mr. Fung was in as much trouble as Suo. His magic sand had spilled down his shirt and his phone was missing. "Ugh! Oh, no! I've lost my marbles!' he screamed, tearing at his seaweed-covered hair.

Jake snickered and yelled, "Well I can see that!" As the two seaweed—and algae-covered "monsters" staggered across the white, snow-covered lawn, a loud waltz began to play, and the people cheered. As the unfortunate relatives crawled into the weeds, the guests laughed and started dancing to the music.

An hour later Mr. Fung, aka the swamp monster, was lying in his recliner. The massager came on, and he groaned in pain as the shiatsu hit a few painful spots. Finding painful spots was no great feat for the machine, as Mr. Fung was simply covered with bruises. "Aaaaah!" he yelled as the machine hit a particularly painful spot. "Those damned kids! To do this to their very own uncle! They'll pay for this!" he snarled and turned the massager off. He heard Suo singing in the shower and yelled, "Suo! Shut up! Can't you see that some people are trying to relax?

The singing stopped, and Suo came out of the shower. "My coffee!" yelled Mr. Fung. Suo ran into the kitchen and returned with a plate piled high with cakes and cookies, plus a large mug of coffee. "Here you are, Dad!" he said as he held out the tray. Suddenly he slipped, and the heavily loaded tray landed on his enraged and shocked father.

"You . . . You brainless, pea-brained . . ." he screamed but then the coffee pot fell over his head and stopped his next words.

Suo looked puzzled. "Dad, how can I be pea-brained if I am brainless? That doesn't make sense!" he said as he scratched his head.

Mr. Fung finally managed to pull the coffee pot off of his head. He staggered into the bathroom to wash in the hot tub. As he went in, he slipped on the wet floor and fell head first into the toilet. He reached up to pull himself out of the smelly water and accidentally flushed it.

Whoosh! went the water. "Urk!" gurgled Mr. Fung after he managed to pull his clean head out of the sucking water. He stumbled backward and toppled into the full hot tub. At that moment Suo peeked in to see what the terrible noises were that were coming out of the bathroom. "Dad! I didn't know that you bathed with your clothes on!" he exclaimed. He watched his groggy father slip out of the hot tub and sprawl onto the floor.

An hour later Mr. Fung lay in his king-size waterbed and sipped on some icy cold, all-natural juice. Suddenly, *blam!* The water bed exploded. Mr. Fung lay on the floor in a puddle of water. "Suo!" he screamed as he grabbed onto a cord. Unfortunately the cord was connected to a radio. *Bonk!* "Ouch!" yelled Mr. Fung. *Blam!* went the lights. "Oof!" went Mr. Fung.

"Bleugh!" wheezed Suo. Five minutes later they were on their way to the hospital. That was the end of their party.

"Jake, Sally! C'mon down! Let's start the lessons early!" called Dad.

"Aw, come on. Who needs this old boring stuff!" whispered Jake. It was Saturday afternoon, and their dad had been inspired again. They had pitched quite a fit six months earlier when Dad had announced his idea at dinner. Now it was time to start the next boring lesson on boring old China.

"Dad, how come I have to sit here in this stuffy room while my friends play? It's school vacation!" Jake argued.

His dad answered him readily. "Because you guys have Emperor Qin Shi Huangdi for a great-great-grandfather! Qin, pronounced like *chin*, gave us the word *China*. The first emperor's name will never die. Qin Shi Huangdi oversaw a standard form of writing so that commands could be read throughout the country. This script has not changed much."

"I don't care who this crazy old King Shit Howdy is, but he sure is one royal pain in the *A*!" mumbled Jake.

"Aw, c'mon! It's not that bad! Besides, it's high time you young people learn your own secret language!" said Dad, trying to liven up the mood. "Now we will start the next lesson on Jon Guo, written 中国 I think. First today we will learn how to say wrong! It is not the new way that you already know but the ancient traditional way! Make a fist and look at it! Look at the cracks! You should see something like the character bu, written 不. You got that? Good! Next, let me teach you how to say dragon. The Dragon was a very important symbol in China, he was the symbol of peace and power. He was written like this 龙. Let me read to you the rest of the dragon lesson! It's on page fifty-two! You may take notes for the quiz in lesson 86. Now as for the text! That will be . . ." A funny look crossed his face. "Now that's weird! I wonder what happened!" He muttered.

"Uh dad? The text you were saying?" said Jake with a ready look. Mr. Wang frowned. "That's just the problem! The text is gone! You wouldn't know anything about it I suppose?"

Jake rolled his eyes. "Yeah sure! Like I would want to study extra!" His dad shrugged and flipped the page. "Anyway let's skip this lesson for now and start lesson 83! Our lesson is on the art of . . ."

Two hours later a figure popped out of the bushed at Uncle Lou's house. "OK! We have found House X! Target gone! Primary obstacle! Penetrating building and locating evidence! Uh, Sally? How *will* we do that?" Asked Jake staring in awe at the huge oaken mansion in front of them. Sally put on a pair of rubber coated gloves and leaped onto the handrail on the porch. Grabbing hold of the gutter she scrambled onto the thin veranda roof. Jumping from window top window and occasionally shinnying up the gutters she made it to the large central dome. Lassoing the steeple in the center she unscrewed the cap and lowered herself to the bottom. She opened the door and dragged in Jake who was staring at the top of the house in awe. "Wow!" he whispered and went in. They searched all the rooms for a hiding place when Sally noticed a dragon painting hanging in the huge starlight room. She looked into the place for the eye and saw the glint on metal in it. Quickly taking a thing titanium wire she twisted it until the head popped out. Reaching in, she found a stack of yellowed papers, a small chest, and in a large manila envelope, the lessons! As she turned around Jake ran in. "Uncle Lou's car just rolled in! You wouldn't believe the wheels on that baby! It's a McLaren!" Sally Grabbed the papers and shoved the chest at Jake. "How could you admire his car when we've just legally committed a burglary? Let's get out of here!" she exclaimed running down the steps. "Hey! You said it was legal! Besides, why are you going down? By now they'll be walking to the front door!" Sally turned and paced the room. What will we do!" she cried in frustration. "Well if you don't mind . . ." said Jake slyly.

"Good-bye Uncle Lou! We love your car!" yelled Jake as the shiny red McLaren sped out of the driveway leaving a bewildered Uncle Lou behind to choke on their dust.

At 7:16 Jake woke up feeling thirsty. He went to the kitchen and drank a glass of water. Suddenly Sally came down. "Jake! We have to go to Valley Sweetwater! There's an important clue there! Hurry! I sold that broken dragon for five thousand dollars to old man Dickens! The supplies are at in that old red wagon. Just get dressed and let's go! Oh yeah, I also put a little surprise in Uncle Lou's house." Jake opened his mouth but Sally pushed him up the stairs. "Go!" she hissed. At Uncle Lou's house the peace and silence of the night woods was shattered by the earsplitting sound of two boxes of fireworks being set off at once. "Suo!!!" came the scream as the house was enveloped in a blinding light.

龙。　龙。　龙。

Uncle Lou Fung was in his bed, sweetly dreaming. Suddenly, his house was bright with light and warning sirens. In his dreams the spotless mountain resort turned an ugly shade of red and became the famous Fuji Yuma volcano erupting. Lou Fung quickly put his clothes on and rushed to his phone, yelling, "Help! There's an eruption underway!" He stepped on a smoke bomb, setting it off, and crashed onto a sprinkler. "Ooow!" he screamed as his robe caught on fire. Being a brilliant man, he immediately rushed to the windows and burst through them. He landed on a sled his thoughtful nephew and niece had left for him. "Aaah!" The sled flew down the street and hit the curb. Uncle Lou flew off and landed head first in a garbage can. Suo, meanwhile, was making a fast getaway on his ten-speed bike. As he raced down the hill he noticed the bike trick festival at the bottom and tried to stop. He applied full brakes, but nothing happened. He screamed as he flew through the entrance at breakneck speed and approached the first ramp. "Aooooo!" he yelled. The judges watched the blur slow down and begin its descent.

As soon as fireworks ended, Sally and Jake rushed to their vessels at the river, jumped in, and started of downriver. After an hour, Sally sighted a cave cleverly hidden by vegetation. They beached the boats and were very surprised to find a boy about sixteen years old crouching there.

"Don't worry, we won't hurt you," Jake called to the boy, who instantly stood up.

"Me, afraid of you? My name's Dave. What's yours?" he grunted.

"I'm Jake, and this is my sister Sally," said Jake

"Now tell me what you're doing here!" Jake and Dave both said at the same. When Jake had explained their whole story, Dave reeled off his own. He told them that his parents had died and that now he had to hunt for food with his bow and arrows. Jake fired off a couple firecrackers just to celebrate their newfound friend.

Then they studied the papers by the light from their campfire. As Sally was putting the biggest dragon back, it fell and broke into twelve pieces. "Oh, Sally what have you done!" exclaimed Jake in horror.

"I didn't mean to!" protested Sally.

"Of course not!" agreed Jake.

"Great!" yelled Sally angrily.

"Are you going to keep on yowling like pigs, or will you shut up?" Dave growled from his sleeping bag. The siblings glared at each other and started picking up the small fragments.

"Look, Jake!" exclaimed Sally. "There's something inside here!"

"What is it?" asked Jake. "Oh, it's just a piece of old paper. What's so exciting about that?" he asked disgustedly.

"Because it's a map, you fog head!" answered Sally proudly.

"Okay. A map of what?" challenged Jake.

"A map of the land!" joked Dave.

"You know, that's not very helpful," said Sally. "Besides, we better stop fooling around if we ever want to get out of here."

"Look," said Jake. "This Chinese character 山 means mountain!"

"Okay, who knows anything about these Chinese mountains?" asked Sally.

"Not me!" said Jake.

"Definitely not me!" said Dave.

"Yeah, I guess you can count me out too," said Sally dejectedly.

"So what are we gonna do?" asked Jake.

"I dunno!" said Dave.

"Does anybody else have ideas?" asked Sally hopefully.

"I don't think so," said Jake

"Neither do I!" added Dave.

So they sat there, thinking what to do. Then Sally spoke up. "Let's just go to bed now and think in the morning," she suggested.

"Good idea!" said Dave.

"Bunkers!" yelled Jake.

They wished each other good night and lay down to sleep. Soon everything was quiet.

龙。　龙。　龙。

The next day they awoke to the sound of their uncle's voice. "Hurry up, you weak-muscled rowers! Bend those backs, use your puny muscles! I've got to catch those kids. They must pay for what they did!"

"Aw, boss! Give us a break!" said one of the slower-witted rowers.

"A break eh? Here's the break of a paddle on your head!" shouted the enraged uncle, breaking the paddle on the unfortunate rower's head.

"Look at that!" said Jake. "I wish we could keep watching them!"

"You can if you follow me," said Dave.

"Really, Dave?" said Sally.

"Really!" said Dave, rolling away a rock to reveal a tunnel.

When they emerged from the tunnel they were on a steep hillside. Looking down, they could see the river rushing by. After five minutes they heard their uncle's voice. "Hurry up, you liver-bellied cowards! Row, row, row this boat quickly down the stream! We will catch those evil kids, though it might take a week!" he sang.

"Boy, what a terrible voice, even for Uncle Lou "Fungi" Fung!" laughed Dave upon hearing the off-key voice.

"I know," answered Sally.

"He's always like that, crabby and off-tone!" joked Jake.

They sat there laughing. Suddenly Dave started slipping down the side of the hill. "Dave!" shouted Sally, and then Dave disappeared beneath the rushing torrent of foaming water.

龙。 龙。 龙。

The water was crystal clear and freezing cold. "Not quite perfect for swimming," Dave thought. Suddenly he was struck with the brilliant idea of swimming Uncle Lou's boat. Under water, he drew out his knife. As he was coming up for a gulp of air, he felt his right leg become trapped in some sort of net. Terrified he tried to free his leg by pulling on it, in vain. Finally he desperately slashed at the net with his knife. As his head rose to the surface he heard the uncle laughing madly. He submerged back under water, swam under the boat, and stabbed it three times. Then he swam against the current toward land. As he pulled himself out of the river, he heard the uproar from the boat. Uncle Lou shrieked, "Where did this water come from?" and then his screams changed to, "Save me! I can't swim!" The rowers threw themselves into the water and swam for shore as the boat and Uncle Lou Fung smashed against the opposite shore. Then the kids heard the sound of a helicopter and were forced to run to the cave to hide.

龙。 龙。 龙。

Mr. Fung awoke, the first thing he saw was his son sitting near him in a soaked chair, crying his head off. His big salty tears ran down his flaming cheeks to the floor. A crying crocodile would look more attractive than his son, though it would probably drown in the puddle that was forming on the floor, Lou Fung thought.

"Did you catch those kids, you big baby?" Lou sneered.

"Uh, no, Dad," his son answered.

"And why not!" the father roared.

"We tried to but we couldn't!" cowered Suo Huei.

"Well, go catch them, and don't come back here until you find them!" seethed Lou.

"O-o-ok-okay, D-Dad!" stuttered a confused Suo as he quickly backed out of the hideout into the valley.

龙。　龙。　龙。

Back in the cave, Sally and Jake were congratulating Dave on his success. "Way to go, Dave!" said Sally

"You were awesome, dude!" added Jake, clapping Dave on his back.

"Oh, it was nothing," answered Dave modestly.

"No, no, no. You were very brave!" said Sally.

"If you keep talking and don't do anything, I'll freeze to death. Then all your praise won't do anything!" admonished Dave.

"Sure, Dave. Jake, help me make a fire!" said Sally.

"Where are the matches?" wondered Jake.

"Here they are!" answered Sally.

"Sally, go bring some firewood," called Jake.

"Why don't you do it?" muttered Sally crossly.

"Stop asking questions and do it!" yelled Jake.

"And what if I don't feel like it?" taunted Sally.

"Then I'll make you!" roared Jake.

"Go ahead and try!" she replied, teasing.

Dave couldn't stand it. "Be quiet, you loud-mouthed goats! One more peep out of you and I'll personally give you each a thrashing! Now make a fire and go to sleep!" he yelled.

At first they glared at each other, but then they made up. "I'm sorry, Jake," said Sally.

"I'm sorry too," said Jake. They shook hands and made a fire. During the night Danny heard an owl, but otherwise everything was quiet.

龙。 龙。 龙。

Meanwhile at Mr. Fung's, six helicopters lifted off to search for the teens. Each patrolled an area of ten acres. The prize for the one who found them was ten grand. As the helicopters roared off, Mr. Fung was planning how to get the information out of them. He decided the best way was through starvation. He laughed evilly, imagining their terrified, hungry looks. Yes, he would make them pay! He would make them pay ten times what they owed him! If only his copters would catch them, he would really make them pay! "Hah! That'll do the trick!" He laughed out loud.

龙。 龙。 龙。

In the third helicopter sat a man called Jonas Ovarian. He was very intent on catching those children. He was determined be the one to catch them. He had to be the one to catch them! Jonas was deeply in debt to Lou—very, very, very deeply in debt. He had even robbed a bank to get enough money, but he had been caught. Yes, he, Jonas Ovarian, had been caught. And that made him very mad. So mad, in fact, that he had taken a risk for dumb Mr. Lou Fung, who was a notorious liar, and headed out in the helicopter to find some silly, useless kids. *Lou better not be lying*, he thought. *He better not be!*

"What was that movement in there? Looked like someone walking!" he said as he landed the chopper on the edge of a cliff.

Jake was gathering firewood. He was on his way back to the cave, when suddenly he was gagged, bound, and thrown into some bushes. The sleeping chemical in the gag began to work, and all he saw next were black circles closing in.

龙。 龙。 龙。

Meanwhile, back at the cave, Sally woke and decided to use the secret tunnel to get a bit of fresh air. As she was walking to the stream for a drink, she heard footsteps coming her way. She peeked around the corner and saw Jonas, but he didn't see her. She started running. As she did she slipped, and a loose rock tumbled down the mountain. She ran faster but felt a dart pierce her arm. Then she saw black. Jonas picked her up, took out the dart, and carried her to the chopper as he had Jake. He took off for China, and radioed the good news to headquarters, smiling grimly to himself upon hearing Uncle Lou Fung's hysterical laughter. Then he reminded the uncle of the prize and that he was expecting it. The reply was, "Don't worry. You'll get your dough in time."

"You better," muttered Jonas. "You better. Ore else you won't see the sun rise tomorrow morning because you will have a knife between your shoulder blades."

龙。 龙。 龙。

Unknown to anybody, Dave had seen everything. He quickly ran back to the cave and took some of the more necessary things with him. Then he beat Jonas back to the copter and hid in the chopper's locker. As he slammed the locker door shut, it locked behind him. He tried unlocking it with a piece of wire but couldn't. Soon Jonas returned with Sally and started the chopper. Dave gave up trying to unlock the locker door and fell asleep.

龙2 RIVER VALLEY

When Sally and Jake awoke, they were in a bamboo cage suspended over a huge stone pit surrounded with carvings of dragons. On the wall was a huge carving of a dragon made out of pure gold and adorned with different jewels. Its ruby eyes glowed and flashed. The room was lit by smaller dragon heads with flames leaping out of their mouths. The pit under them was smeared with soot and emitted a horrible smell. All around the room were frightful instruments and weapons. They knew, without question, that they were in a torture chamber. The door opened. In strode an old man magnificently robed in yellow clothes, shoes, and jewels. Everything he wore was yellow. Behind him came a younger man, about eighteen years old, whose manner was that of a prince. Then came a woman and two more children. Behind them strode guards and nobles. And who should they see but Uncle Lou, smiling smugly like a cat with two fish. Then Sally noticed that Dave wasn't anywhere to be seen.

"I wonder where Dave is?" she whispered to Jake.

Jake frowned and shook his head. "Come to think of it, I have no idea!" he said. Sally looked worried. Then a very nervous man rushed in. He cleared his throat and shouted in Chinese, "Bow down to Emperor Chui Hang Li, ruler of the Empire of the Golden Dragon, the sun, and the morning star! Let every knee bow down low before his magnificence!"

As soon as he had finished, everyone, even the prince, bowed down and cried, "Live long, oh emperor of the sun and the rising star! May the days of your mighty rule last forever!"

Sally looked at Jake and muttered, "I didn't know emperors even existed! I wonder what country we are in? I sure doubt this is America!" Jake nodded and opened his mouth to speak, but a man who looked like a general roared, "Silence!"

Then the emperor looked at the man who had shouted, nodded, and spoke just four words, "Where is the elixir?

Sally crossed her arms and glared at the emperor! "Hah! As if we know!" Jake spat on the floor and shook the bars. "Lou! As soon as I get out of here you are history!" Mr. Fung rubbed his chin. "Oh, but you won't be getting out of here! At least . . . not for quite a while!" The Emperor looked at the blood smeared room and sniffed disdainfully. Then he left, ushered out by the fanfare of foreign instruments. All the people filed out until just twelve remained. One was Lou, one was the man who had shouted "Silence!" and the others were samurais. The strange man was called Nian Hei, which meant dark year. He picked up a torch and walked over to the siblings. Scowling, he thrust the torch into the pit. "Tomorrow we start the lessons!" he said grinning menacingly. Nian picked up a heavy ax and twirled it, driving it into a block of wood. Then he poured some oil into the pit below. The oil burned, sending up gusts of smelly smoke. He laughed as they coughed and cleared their eyes. Then he stretched and walked out of the cave.

Uncle Lou followed, smiling to himself. "Revenge is mine! Those useless little relatives of mine will pay!" he thought. "Dismissed!" he barked at the samurais and glided away.

龙。 龙。 龙。

Back at the chopper, Dave was awake. He went back to work on the lock and was soon free. He quickly gathered the supplies and jumped out of the helicopter. He took off at a sprint and ran toward what looked like a rock face. When he got there he found an opening behind a bush. Since it looked safe and dry, he crept inside through a narrow and crooked tunnel. When his eyes had adjusted to the darkness, he saw that he was in some sort of cave with a narrow passage at the top. He also heard a river, and he found a rather large crack in the wall that allowed him to see a low, wide passage. After a quick crawl he found a wide river. As he knelt down to drink, he felt a stalactite next to him. While he drank, he heard a waterfall further down the river. He shuddered at the thought of falling in the river and being swept over the waterfall. He went back to the cave and climbed up a rope to explore a passage by the roof. It turned out to be a chimney that could be used as an escape hatch. He climbed down, set up camp, and lit a campfire. By the time he was finished it was three in the morning.

Then he decided to try and rescue his friends. He put on the samurai sword along with his bow and arrows and raced to the helicopter to put on a flight suit. Then he casually walked past the sleeping guards, who were snoring loudly, and went to explore the cave.

As he was walking past a chamber, he noticed that it was guarded. He crept noiselessly past the sleeping guards and saw his friends suspended in a bamboo cage from the ceiling, sleeping. He climbed up to the cage and opened it. Then he woke his sleeping friends and helped them down. Then Dave got an idea. "Let's put the guards into the cage and see how they like it!" he whispered. They strode into the hall, and noiselessly tied the guards with a rope. Then they dragged them and the cage outside. They suspended the cage over the cliff and put the guards in it. When they crept past the same cavern where they had been imprisoned, Sally accidentally tripped and bumped into a big vase, which fell down and shattered with a crash.

The kids froze and heard their uncle yelling and coming toward them. Some guards approached from another direction, and the kids were forced to go back to the same room where Jake and Sally had recently been imprisoned. Again Sally tripped, and she fell against the throat of the dragon. To their surprise, it swung inward. They looked at one another and quickly jumped inside. Then they shut the door and crawled quickly down the tunnel. Off to the side was a big, wide tunnel, but they passed it, as it smelled damp. When they had reached the end, they saw the same room in which they had been, but this time they were inside the carved dragon's mouth. They smiled and made themselves comfortable, as if they were about to watch a movie. They watched as the guards tumbled in and shouted the alarm, and their uncle barreled in. They watched as he ranted and raved at the guards for not watching carefully enough. Then their uncle leaned on a block of stone near the corner of the room and as it suddenly gave way he fell inside. Dave grabbed a torch, and they immediately rushed off into the big tunnel they had just passed at a run.

After running for fifteen minutes, the kids noticed the ancient Chinese characters above each of the side doorways. Dave saw a sign that said 感, which means feel. They went in, and when the passage split, Jake saw a sign. He called Dave and asked him to read it. The sign said 感岁末你 到 那 个 祝 你 不 到 这 个. Dave explained, "Roughly, this says that we will see our end if we go this way. But it also suggests we don't go that way. He leaves us with only one option, and that is going back." The kids looked at one another and ran back out of the tunnel to the main one. Just when it seemed they couldn't go any farther, Dave sighted a sign over one of the doorways that said 水. Since that meant water and they were all thirsty, they turned into the side tunnel and soon spotted a wild, foaming underground river. They quickly took a drink and blew up the inflatable raft. But as soon as they were done the guards came racing up. The teens quickly shoved of and were soon lost from sight. However the guards had seen them and blew up inflatable rafts of their own. They too, soon were off down the river. As they were speeding along, the kids heard the terrible sound of a waterfall plunging off into the abysses of the earth ahead. Jake and Sally screamed in fright, while Dave chuckled loudly. "What are you laughing at?' screamed Jake. "We're all about to die, and all you do is laugh! Why, you deserve to be tossed overboard!"

"Are you sure?" asked Dave mischievously. "Well, then, maybe you don't want to paddle to the left?"

"To the left? Okay, but don't blame me when we go over the waterfall!" Jake muttered. When he threw the rope with the lasso on the end and pulled them to safety, Dave smiled smugly at their amazed faces. "How did you do that!" asked Jake in an amazed voice.

"I'll explain when we make camp," promised Dave.

龙。 龙。 龙。

Uncle Lou Fung had gone in the first boat, and now he regretted it. He did not feel very brave as he sped toward the waterfall. He tried lassoing the banks but couldn't make fast to anything. Finally, in desperation, he kicked all the supplies overboard and put on a lifejacket, though he doubted it would help. As he neared the waterfall, he screamed and disappeared over the falls. The other guards suffered the same fate as their boss. The last thing Lou Fung remembered was a pain in his head. Then he was in a world of silence and darkness.

One of Lou's most greedy and brainless guards saw him go under and grabbed him by the collar. Then he pulled Mr. Fung onto a raft and climbed on himself. The guard, whose name was Chang, was one of the five guards who got out of the tunnel. The rest either drowned or were left clinging to or lying on the ledges. Meanwhile, Chang sighted light and got ready to paddle for shore. He didn't care about Lou, but he did care about the money he would get for saving Lou Fung, who in his great and wonderful wisdom had decided to follow these useless kids. Oh, how Chang would have loved to dump Lou Fung overboard, but greed got the better of him.

Soon the boat was out in the open in some sort of valley, surrounded by mountains. Chang paddled to shore and made camp. His eyes glistened, and he drooled at the thought of the reward he would receive for his service. Caught up in his thoughts of money, Chang forgot that

Lou Fung almost never parted with his money, and he did not realize he would probably be lied to and never receive a single penny.

Back at the cage, the sleeping guards woke up and started screaming for help. Jonas, recognizing the situation in an instant, quickly came up and hid in some bushes, while the rest of the guards rushed toward the cave. Finding the hole in the wall they rushed in; upon reaching the main tunnel, they thundered off. By then, Jonas had entered the main cavern. Seeing no one, he took all the money in Lou's safe and ran outside. He got inside the helicopter and lifted off, heading for a hidden cabin in the Grand Canyon.

Back at the cave, the children had awoken. Dave started a fire and cooked breakfast. As the trio ate, they made plans for the day. "Let's go hunting in the cliffs!" suggested Jake.

"Nah, we have enough food for now," answered Dave lazily.

Then Sally spoke up. "Let's go exploring! It's better than Jake's idea, and its fun!"

"Good idea! Plus we could also get to know the territory," commented Dave.

"Let's do that!" enthused Jake. So after breakfast, off they went on an exploration trip. As Sally was walking along, she heard a small bleating voice. She quickly hurried toward it, and soon she saw an injured goat, lying at the bottom of a small cliff. Sally quickly called the others and begged them to help her carry the goat to the cave. Reluctantly they did, but not without some grumbling.

"You and your little pets!" laughed Jake, but Sally was too preoccupied to hear him.

Later Dave went out to bring some grass for the goat to eat, and he returned with a little surprise.

"Look what I got you, Sal!" he teased her.

"Come on, give me the grass!" said Sally, not looking up from the goat. Dave gave her the grass and revealed a hawk with an injured wing.

"I guess I'll take care of this one. After all, hawks are cool, aren't they?" asked Jake.

"Yeah, I guess so," yawned Dave.

"Good, you're not interested! I have the hawk all to myself, and nobody else!" said Jake gleefully.

"For your information, that's a falcon, *not* a hawk," Dave said knowingly.

"Hawk or falcon, why should I care? All I know is that I'm calling him Swift, in honor of my favorite story character, Tom Swift. Man, that's one brave guy!" sighed Jake.

"That's right. You want to be Tom Swift and lose your favorite sister!" laughed Sally, punching Jake playfully in the arm..

Laughing, Jake went back to nursing the falcon's wing, and Sally fixed the goat's leg, while Dave slept away.

Back at Chang's camp, Uncle Lou had awoken. He moaned and groaned at the pain in his head and asked how he got there. So Chang told him some of the real story, with quite a few differences, however, that he thought would make the uncle give him a bigger prize. One of the flowery lies he told was that he had shot the children, who had been swept away down the waterfall, never to be seen again. Mr. Fung and twenty-six men were the remaining survivors until a helicopter drop brought more replacements. They ate whatever they could find, and then they lay down to sleep, leaving one man to guard them while they slept. Uncle Lou lay down and grinned at the sky, caught up in his selfish thoughts of finding the elixir. He thought of the money and fame, not to mention the prolonged life, he would soon be master of finally sleep overcame his tired body, and he fell into a dreamless sleep, forgetting his own boss's orders.

The next morning Lou sent out scouts to discover their position. Then he sent the rest out to go hunting. He ordered the guards to entertain him, which they did. The uncle laughed harshly at their attempts to amuse him. The guards did not like being laughed at, but they had no choice. The hunters arrived with only two sparrows, which barely made a mouthful. Uncle Lou ate one himself and gave the other one to Chang. Then he sent the guards out again, along with threats to bring more or go hungry. The guards grumbled but obeyed for fear of starving. They spent four more days in that fashion before an unexpected turn of events came by.

Back at the children's camp, the hawk had fully recovered, and the goat was on the road to recovery. On the second morning, Sally asked Jake where the maps and clues were. Jake answered, "I don't know. I thought you had them all along!"

"And I thought you had them!" she exclaimed.

Then Jake stiffened and said, "I guess our uncle has them in his bag."

"Well, we're going to get them back, and we're leaving today!" decided Sally.

"But we can't! We'll drown!" yelped Jake.

"Then I'll go by myself," said his sister determinedly.

Finally Jake agreed. "At least I'll have my conscience clear of you!" he said, resigned. They released the hawk and put the goat in the canoe.

Sally and Jake sat with the goat in the canoe, while Dave sat in the rubber boat with the supplies. Suddenly they heard the familiar roar of a waterfall. Jake grimaced. As he gritted his teeth, the boat tipped and went over the edge. The waterfall plunged underground again, and as they fell, Jake grabbed hold of the sides. When they landed they found themselves in a long line of rapids that boiled over huge rocks and disappeared into twenty foot wide holes. Just as they thought it couldn't get worse, they heard a steady sucking sound. It grew louder and louder. Suddenly Dave, who was in front, screamed, "Paddle to the left! The left! On the right is a huge sucker hole!"

Sally's eyes widened as she saw the huge hole that would be upon them in a minute. It pulled in everything that came close to it to the bottom of the river. Jake saw a huge rock ahead. He paddled toward it, and when they hit it, he shoved off as hard as he could with the rifle. The rifle broke in two, and Jake had to drop it. They were on the edge of the river, and it seemed that they were out of danger, but no! A hole that took up half the river steadily drew them into itself, then faster and faster. Suddenly the canoe hit something and was spit out of the hole with such force that it almost overturned.

While they floated, they checked for damages. Dave yelled that a box of supplies, the rifle, and most of the bullets were missing. All of them were drenched and shivering. Dave had almost overturned, and the goat was frightened out of his wits. Even worse, they didn't know if they would see daylight again. While Sally comforted the goat, Jake battled the waves as Dave had shown him. Finally they could see a tiny speck of light ahead through the darkness of the tunnel, and everybody cheered. "Never loved light more than now!" exclaimed Sally.

"You can say that again!" added Jake, laughing out loud.

Further down, the tired children saw a crack in the darkness. As they approached it, it became bigger and brighter, and finally their canoe whooshed out into the valley. Their eyes were not adjusted to the sunshine, and for a couple of seconds they were blinded by the outside light. When they could finally see, they were breathless with the wonderful scene their eyes beheld.

In Uncle Lou's camp, everyone was sleeping soundly except for a guard named Fu Ching, who was sitting on a log sharpening an oak branch into a spear to frighten off animals. He stood up and listened to the darkness of the night, in case anything came too close. Then the man sat back down and started making arrows. He sat and waited, for he had to be ready to escape tomorrow night so he would finally be free from his crazy boss's stupid rules and awful diet. It was the only reason he had volunteered to be night guard and give up sleep. So Fu Ching kept on, and he missed the restful sleep he needed, all for the freedoms that he wanted.

They passed Uncle Lou's camp quietly. Beaching the craft about two miles down from Uncle Lou, the kids made camp in a crevice. They sat there eating some dried food and discussing plans for a raid on the camp they had passed. Jake spoke first. "Maybe we should make a surprise attack!" he suggested.

"Nah, that's too noisy," countered Dave.

"So what?" argued Jake.

"It's too dangerous, and that's that!" said Dave firmly.

Then Sally spoke up. "Let's just quietly take their food, guns, and other necessities and run away!"

"What about taking a spear to scare any guards with?" suggested Jake.

"It's okay, I guess." answered Dave halfheartedly.

"Let's do it then!" decided Sally.

So half an hour later they split up in the bushes and crept slowly into the camp. Jake ran into the camp and only then realized that a man was guarding the camp. Fu Ching jumped up to yell, only to get butted in the rear end. He flew through the air, hit a rock with his head, and sank to the ground. Jake almost yelled as a shadow came at him, but then he realized that it was only Sally.

"How did he do that!" whispered Jake, amused by what his sister's goat was capable of.

"Oh, it was nothing," Sally whispered back. "You see, he had a soft rear end!" she joked.

Then Dave came in, and even he had a smile in his eyes for the funny goat. "That was pretty good!" he whispered at Sally. Then they quickly gathered p the rogues' equipment and hurried back to camp.

At camp, Sally petted and praised the goat, giving him extra food. She gave him a name, Rag Boy, or Raggie. The goat had fully recovered and now went outside for solo walks, but he always returned when Sally called to him.

As they sat around the fire talking, they heard a noise outside the crevice. They crawled out, with Jake holding the .22 rifle. They saw a wolf running at them. Sally almost screamed, but Dave quieted her. As the wolf came into shooting range, Dave fired at it. The wolf yelped but kept going. Dave fired at it three more times, and it kept running.

Sally grabbed the gun from Dave and braced for a hit. "Hey! You can't do that! Give it back!" shouted Dave. "Give me the gun! Now!" he demanded, but Sally completely ignored him. When the wolf came close enough, she cracked him on the head. The wolf staggered and then fell on its side, unconscious. In shock, Jake looked at the wolf at his feet and scratched his head. "Way to go, sis! That was one heck of a swing! Maybe you'll make it to the league someday!" he said, clapping her on the back. Sally grinned and threw the gun on the floor. First they congratulated Sally on her quick thinking and then discussed what to do with the wolf.

"Let's eat it!' proposed Jake keeping a straight face. "Sure! But you eat first!" said Sally with a grimace.

Jake grinned and looked at the skin. "It sure would look nice on you Sally! Pretty coat!" Sally rolled her eyes. "You call this flea-bitten animal 'pretty'? I can't find a clean spot on it and you want me to *wear* it?!" Dave laughed. "Well we certainly can't keep it! It would eat Sally's goat and both of you and then have me and the hawk er, sorry Jake, *falcon* for desert!" Jake rubbed his belly. Come to think of it Maybe I *should* have the goat for desert! Maybe the hindquarters?" Sally jumped up. "You just try and the next thing you know that goat will be having its first snack since who knows when!" Jake sighed. "Duh! I was just kidding, I mean seriously, have that disgusting mongrel in your belly?! It doesn't even have any meat on it!"

Just then, Rag Boy, who had been attracted to the long underwear hanging on a line, jumped out of the bush and charged the hanging underwear, in the process snagging a cowboy hat on his horn. That frightened the already terrified guards even more and sent Lou right back into the same tree from which the underwear had come. The kids burst with silent laughter.

"Help! It's Joe Buck's ghost!"

"No, it isn't! It's Larry Cullman's ghost!"

"You're both wrong! It isn't either of them! I recognized him, and it was the Lone Ranger himself!"

Upon the word ghost the orderly camp turned into a madhouse.

"Help me, I see him!" shouted one.

"There he is! On the left!" yelled another.

"No, he's on the right!" screeched somebody else.

"There's the ghost!"

"No! That's my underwear drying off!"

"I've caught him! I've caught him! I've . . . oomph!"

"Hey! Wait a second, that's Albert Avon! Not Harry Wilkes!"

"Harry Wilkes?! Where?! I killed his brother last summer!"

In the middle of this, the very frightened Uncle Lou Fung scurried up a tree. All the talk about ghosts terrified him, and he showed what a coward he truly was. "Help me! I want my mo . . . wait a second—no, I don't! I need my gun, not my mommy! Bring me a gun!" he bawled into the night. But nobody heard him above the uproar.

Finally Fu Ching heard him and went to his aid. "What do you need a gun for? A gun we don't even have!"

"To ward off ghosts!" whimpered Uncle Lou.

"Ghosts? Ghosts! Have you completely lost your mind to believe that nonsense? That was no ghost that hit me, or my name isn't Fu Gao Ching!"

"It wasn't?" sniffed Uncle Lou, wiping away his tears.

"Of course it wasn't!" sighed Fu Ching.

"Why don't you tell them that?" puzzled Lou.

"You want to try? Ya think someone there'll believe you? In your dreams!" sneered Fu. Shame-faced, Lou returned to the camp to restore order and think about how to punish that nosy Fu Ching for lowering him in that clump of trees.

Fung Ching, however, had other ideas. "Why not eliminate Mister Lou Fung for good?" he thought. "It should be easy enough. Besides, everybody hates him, so what's the point of letting him live? It'll have to be soon, though, or he might suspect me." And with his plans, things might have gotten ugly if not for one thing.

The three friends and their pets had just stepped out of their makeshift home and were lightly sprinting down the valley trail.

Approaching their uncle's camp, they found it from the noise rather than by sight. They quickly hid behind a scrawny bush and listened to the uproar. "Ghost alert, ghost alert!" someone yelled. "Shut up!" yelled someone else. And then to the children's delight they saw a very sheepish and angry Uncle Lou hobbling into the camp. "Calm down, calm down! There's nothing to be afraid of! The ghost is gone. I scared him away!" proclaimed Lou.

"Sheesh! Just listen to that fraud cat mumbling away!" laughed Sally.

To make matters worse for Lou, Swift the hawk became entangled in a white nightshirt and landed next to Uncle Lou, who was already frightened out of his wits. Uncle Lou's eyes grew round; he screamed bloody murder, and then he fainted. Jake and Dave leaped up and caught the falling Uncle Lou, while Sally tried to secretly catch the goat. The frightened guards ran off, screaming into the night, and did not even notice that their leader was missing.

Fu Ching was also running away from the camp, even though he was not afraid of any ghosts attacking him. Unlike the other guards, he had taken supplies to support him on his way. He was running quickly into the night, chuckling, when a white figure bounded toward him. Before he could even scream, it was upon him, and Fu was bowled over as something hit him full in the stomach, hard. Fu lost consciousness before Sally appeared. When she saw the white figure lying on the ground, at first she thought it was her pet goat, until she noticed the Rag Boy standing by a tree nearby eating grass. She unrolled the figure wrapped in the cloth. When she saw Fu Ching, she tied him up and dumped him in the bushes to get Jake's help and take him to Dave for show and tell later.

The boys considered what to do with Lou. "Let's take him to a cliff and leave him in a canyon until he confesses!" joked Jake.

"You know, that's not a bad idea," answered Dave, thoughtfully rubbing his chin.

"What?" exclaimed Sally, emerging from behind a bush. "Have you guys actually lost your minds?"

"Why, no! I think we were just kidding!" laughed Dave.

"Hey, guys, guess who this is!" smirked Sally.

"Uh, who? The president?" mocked Dave.

"Of course not, dummy. It's one of the guards!" corrected Sally.

"Well, well, now! Look at that, Lou *and* his guard! Now who woulda thought of that!" exclaimed Jake.

"Okay, guys, here's the plan. Let's dump this guard next to the river, all nice and wrapped, just like a Christmas present. And Uncle Lou too. When they wake up, we'll follow them," decided Dave.

"Aw, come on. I wanted to have a little bit of fun with them before they left!" groaned Jake, pretending to be disappointed.

"Okay now! Let's do this quick before these guys wake up! Raggie can help us. Now get moving!" barked Sally. And with those words, they stood up and got to work, mumbling all the way.

About an hour later Uncle Lou woke up. "Where am I?" he groaned. He looked around and recognized where he was. He set off in the direction where the camp was. When he arrived there, he saw Fu soothing the guards, "That's all right, that's all right. He won't come back—he's dead!" All the guards cheered. Furiously Lou stormed into camp.

"*Oh,* won't he, *Fu,* you traitor! So that's what you say when I'm gone! Well, I'll put a stop to this rumor!" he screamed, grabbing a stick and whacking Fu Ching on the head. Fu yelled and fell down, holding his head.

"Ow, ow, ow! Help me, mates! I'm being murdered!" he shouted, but the guards sat frozen while Lou beat Fu. Finally he stopped and spat out between clenched teeth, "Well? Is that enough, or would you like some more?"

"Enough, enough! Spare me, I beg you! My wrists still hurt from rubbing against the tree when I scraped off the ropes!" Fu moaned, holding on to his head.

"Get up, you filthy hogs! Quit starin' and get to work!" said Lou, directing his anger at the other guards. "We're leaving now! Our boss lives near here, and we'll be safe there! Pack up quickly and stand in double columns!" When they were ready Uncle Lou bellowed, "March quickly now! Left, right, left, right! Down the path we go!"

And so they went marching out of camp, Fu hobbling along at the back and cursing Lou through his teeth.

Dave, who had watched it all, quickly ran to their crevice camp, informed the others about what had happened, and started packing up. As soon as they had finished, they ran to catch up with Lou's party. When they found the guards marching and singing loudly, they settled along about two hundred feet behind them. Soon they were talking and joking quietly.

"Ya know, I heard a story once about this guy who had a really mean wife. She was so mean that when she ordered pair of silver earrings, she ranted when he brought home diamond ones! So this man went with her to the desert to a very deep well far, far, away to get rid of her. By the time they got there, his wife was already complaining about being thirsty. So he helped her down, and when she leaned over the well to grab the bucket, he shoved her over the edge into the water! Of course, she cursed him and screamed for about two days. He ignored her. By the fourth day she was calm as a kitten and begging to be pulled out. So the man pulled her out. And when he did he tied the bucket to her foot in secret! So when she threw a tantrum again, he yanked the rope and she flew back into the well! D'you know how it ended?" asked Dave.

"Naw . . . how?" said Jake eagerly.

"He tied the rope to her leg again and tied the other end to his camel, so she had no way of stopping or complaining loudly enough! By the time he got home, her stubbornness was gone! Neat, huh?" laughed Dave.

"C'mon! Enough with stories! Someone tell me a joke!" exclaimed Sally.

"Okay! What is black and blue all over, except it has a couple red stripes on its body?" asked Jake mischievously.

"Uh, a porpoise that has been bitten by a shark?" asked Sally.

"Nope!" answered Jake.

Now it was Dave's turn to guess. "A swallow with red paint on its back?" he guessed.

"Wrong again!" smiled Jake.

"What is it then? Stop teasing and tell us!" prodded Sally impatiently.

"One of the guards after he gets a beating from Uncle Lou!" Jake crowed triumphantly.

"Wrong! It's when Lou gets a beating from his boss!" giggled Sally. Then they all laughed together, not realizing how close those words were to the deadly truth.

龙3 In the Throat of the Golden Dragon

Time is the most precious treasure when there's shortage of it. The way was dangerous and unfamiliar all the way. The sun was quickly moving toward the horizon, trying to hide behind the mountains as soon as possible. Dave, Jake, and Sally were worried about when Lou would stop to camp.

"What if he never does?" joked Jake.

"Of course he will, you silly boy!" said Sally good-naturedly. By now she didn't sound so perky. After that they walked in silence, thinking about their quest.

Just as they were getting desperate to stop and rest, Uncle Lou slowed his little band a bit and ordered the soldiers to be on the alert for good camping spots. The teens sighed in relief and also looked for their own spot to camp. Then there came a shout from up ahead. "There's a small clearing down this ridge where we can make a good camp!"

"Very well, it'll have to do," decided Lou Fung. The guards rushed forward joyfully, and soon the path was empty.

"Whew!" gasped Jake as he sank down on a log, "If we had gone one more foot, I would have dropped down dead, wolves or not!"

"Sorry to disappoint you, but in case you have forgotten, we have to find and make camp, tired or not," said Dave wearily.

"All right then, let's get started! Dave, I saw a good spot back there a while ago. Now quickly run over there and check it out!" ordered

Sally in a crisp tone. Those weeks of training in the gym. While the two boys were dead tired, Sally had barely broken a sweat. "Jake, you start following Dave, and if the spot is okay, pitch up camp and start a fire. I've got to find dinner," she said and then disappeared into the bushes.

In the morning at the guards' camp, Fu had become insane with a mad desire to kill Uncle Lou. In fact, he was so desperate that he had decided to kill Lou that very morning. He took some death berries and mixed them in Lou's drink. Lou picked his cup up and took a sip. Before he could swallow, a guard brought him bad news.

"Sir!" he began. "We have spotted a chopper with a police symbol on its side, and we are waiting for further orders." He saluted Lou so hard he almost blacked out.

"What!" Lou choked, spitting out the poisonous drink quickly. *A helicopter so close can only mean that they suspect something!* he quickly thought. "Uh, yes, yes!" he stammered. "Tell the others to pack up and hide in the bushes by the roadside!"

Then he quickly ran off to hide.

The kids had also noticed the police. They packed up and hid in the bushes to avoid detection—not from the police but from the milling guards, who were also in the bushes.

In the chopper sat Mike Lamar. He was a sergeant from the China Air Police Force. He thought he had seen something moving in the clearing in a copse of bushes, but he didn't see anything now. He decided he had been seeing things and turned the copter around. "Patrol number 45 coming in. Position oh, 45 North-east in the Ural Mountains, slightly west of Mount Keskubatchi. No suspicious behavior anywhere. Roger that." he reported to headquarters by radio.

"I read you, 45, loud and clear. So Patrol 53 must have been wrong about that smoke coming from your patrol area. All right, all clear. Continue patrolling, and report anything out of the ordinary to headquarters. Over and out," came the reply. Mike shrugged and flew on. Suddenly he saw a man standing on a cliff. It was Fu, whose brain had finally snapped. When Mike picked him up, Fu didn't resist and just giggled foolishly. When Mike tried to radio his finding to headquarters, he was interrupted by a call. "A man has escaped from a prison car. All patrols, be on alert." Mike smiled at the crazy man and said, "Maybe you don't know this, old man, but you're my only hope of a promotion. Don't worry. I'm sure they'll send you to a nice nursing home!" he assured the crazed Fu.

As soon as the chopper had gone, Lou leaped out of the bushes and ordered the guards to move on. "One, two, three, four! One, two, three, four!" They marched off, with the children following sleepily behind them. As they marched, Uncle Lou began to feel a slight headache, which was followed by a stomachache. He shrugged it off, assuming he had eaten something bad. Later he began to puzzle about why he couldn't find Fu Ching. But then he decided that he was glad Fu was missing and that it was just as well that he had disappeared.

The teens saw Lou marching and followed him from behind.

"Has he gone crazy? What sort of idiot goes out into the middle of nowhere with an army around him?" wondered Jake.

Sally sighed and said, "What kind of idiot steals mail, lies, and cheats?"

"Good point," muttered Jake.

But just an hour later, Lou's pain increased to such an extent that he had to be carried. Finally he managed to wheeze out, "Stop for camp . . . I . . . don't feel . . . good . . ."

The general saluted and marched off. A minute later the marching stopped, and the soldiers pitched camp. Lou tried to stand up and fainted from the pain.

"Huh? Why'd he stop now?" wondered Jake.

Sally groaned and said, "You're gonna have to find out yourself!"

They spent the whole day resting and drinking from a stream. It seemed wonderful to have at least one day to enjoy a rest. But by the second day they'd had enough of resting.

"I know!" exclaimed Jake. "Let's explore that valley below us!" he said, pointing to the valley below.

"But what if Uncle Lou starts moving?" said Sally worriedly.

"Or what if we get lost?" mentioned Dave.

"Bah! Of course we won't get lost!" laughed Jake.

"Well . . . Okay!" decided Sally. "We still need some exercise."

Then they all turned into worker bees, packing up.

Soon all was ready, and they walked into the valley. On one side was an endless field with high grass. On the other was a vast jungle. High above them towered majestic snow-peaked mountains. It was awe-aspiring. Standing by the river dividing the jungle from the field, the teens could see all of this beauty. "This is so cool!" whispered Jake, hiking down the river. Down in the valley it was a humid ninety degrees.

"Hey, I know! Let's go swimming!" said Jake. So they spent the afternoon splashing in the clear river. Jake and Dave took a long vine from the jungle and tied it to a tree leaning over the river. They climbed up a tall rock and flew over the water. When they had reached the climax of the swing, they let go and splashed into the sparkling, blue river. Then Dave noticed a tall cliff overhanging the water. "Hey!" he shouted, "Let's dive off of that cliff!" Jake was unsure of this but followed him after Dave splashed in first.

Sally swam a bit but then went to explore the jungle for food carrying the shotgun. She returned, triumphant, with a basket full of fruit. 'Where'd you get the basket?" asked Jake, puzzled.

"I made it!" said Sally proudly.

"You made it! How?" exclaimed Dave.

"Grandma taught me!" explained Sally, unloading the fruit. While they ate Sally told the boys about some ruins she had found in the middle of the jungle. They were very big, and some parts of it were quite okay. "Maybe we could camp there?" she asked. Dave nodded, his mouth too full of mango to speak. Then Sally took out two parts of an old broken spear. "Look!" she exclaimed.

Dave whistled, impressed at the find. "That might come in handy!" he said, examining the spear. Suddenly he froze. "Why, it's hollow!" he exclaimed. Jake looked surprised. Suddenly he grabbed the spear and smashed it on a nearby tree.

Dave was shocked. "Why'd you do that!" he demanded angrily. "I could have fixed it!" Jake ignored him and picked up the piece of paper that had fluttered out of the spear. He read the words:

ALL OF THE TRAPS I'VE LAID SO FAR,
CAN OPEN BUT ONE WORD!
PRESS QIN HUANGDI AND YOU ARE FREE,
IT'LL OPEN ANY DOOR!

Jake frowned and shook his head. Then he handed it to Sally, who put it in her backpack. The boys spent some more time splashing until Jake discovered he had some water goggles. So he and Dave studied the beautiful fish near the cliff. Dave caught one. That reminded them of fishing, so they made fishing sticks and tied thin but sturdy vines to the end. Then they caught a few bugs and got onto a rock. Dave caught two salmon and a trout, but poor Jake caught only a minnow. Just as he was about to give up, he felt a big pull. Finally, after fifteen minutes of fighting, he pulled out a big largemouth bass. Happy, they returned to shore. They gave the fish to Sally and went to get fruit and possibly meat. Jake did manage to get a pheasant, but despite practicing, he couldn't get anything else. He had only wounded the pheasant, so Dave said that that was just as well. He built a small cage for it and threw it the leftover bugs from fishing. The bird was upon them in an instant. Then the three friends sat down to eat a delicious dinner of baked fish and fruit. After that, full and contented, they lay down to sleep.

In the morning they woke up bright and early to start the new day. They killed the pheasant and cooked it. Then Sally again mentioned the ruins she had seen the day before. "Let's visit them!" she suggested.

"Okay!" agreed Jake. "If Dave agrees, I'll go too!" he added looking at Dave.

Dave smiled and laughed. "Well, what can I say? Let's get ready!" he said, picking up the shotgun. Jake and Sally also started getting ready to move.

Soon they entered the forest. "Hey! It's pretty dark in here!" said Jake. Dave also mentioned the strange darkness they walked along for a while. Sally said they were almost there, and suddenly it grew totally dark. Their stunned silence was broken by a scream that cut the darkness.

"W-what is i-it?" asked Sally, fearful. Jake was too shocked to reply. Suddenly the darkness exploded in a ball of fire! Ahead of them rose a mighty fireball. Then it disappeared, and they could see the sun once more.

"I think that's called an eclipse!" said Dave in awe. "But what was that huge fireball doing here in the wilderness!" he asked, still adjusting to the light. Dave shrugged and started walking. "We'll find out when we get there!" he said over his shoulder. Sally hesitated but then moved forward. Jake followed with a drawn bow. *Lucky I made this!* he thought. Sally drew her knife.

After five minutes they were faced with a dense wall of vegetation. Jake took the samurai sword and swung at the wall. The blade bit into the plants but then hit something solid. Excitedly, Jake drew his buck knife and slashed at the greenery. In a few seconds the sturdy knife had made an opening that revealed wood. Five minutes later they uncovered the bottom part of a huge gate covered with bronze dragons. Dave frowned and loaded his gun at the sight of the new padlock and chains on the other side. Jake didn't even hesitate. With a yell he ran at the gate and slashed through both the padlock and the chains. Then he shoved his well-trained shoulder at the gate, and with a creak it swung open. Cautiously they sneaked in. The walls were ten feet thick and forty feet tall. "Holy cow! These things are monstrous!" whispered Jake, in awe. Once inside, they found themselves on a rough road leading in three directions. Jake looked at all of them and chose the one that led forward. In a few minutes they entered a temple. Somewhere close by they heard strange music. It sounded eerie in this seemingly abandoned place. Then from behind a door came a man who was dressed like a priest. He carried a pole with a dragon head on top.

"Man, you would think they actually worship dragons here!" muttered Jake.

"They do!" whispered Dave grimly. Sally gasped as a mouse ran by her. The priest whirled around and gave the entire room a through look. Then he scrutinized the ceiling. Finally he shrugged and walked on. Jake let out the breath he had been holding and crept to another entrance leading deeper into the heathen temple. Sally was so worried she didn't notice where she was going. Suddenly she tripped over a statue and bumped into another one. It crashed to the floor and broke into pieces. There came a yell, and a priest appeared behind them. His eyes grew wide and he drew his saber, screaming. Jake whirled and slashing a rope, dropping a heavy velvet curtain on the priest. Then he and the others ran to the big room ahead. In the room were three doors. One had smoke pouring out of it. The other was in ruins. And only choice that seemed possible was cut off when a horde of samurais leaped out of it. Sally gave a shriek as *shiruken* stars whizzed around them. Jake slashed at one, cutting it in half, and batted another away. Then he darted into the half-ruined tunnel and scrambled over the first rock. Sally and Dave followed, ducking the sharp projectiles. Just as they caught up with Jake, the first samurai gave a ninja scream and somersaulted over the wall. "Whoa! Ninjas! I can handle soldiers, but I don't know if my skills can match these guys!" Jake said and ran on as the ninja/samurai poured into the hole in the wall.

Jake was becoming tired and frightened when he saw a weak light ahead of him. The distance between the guards decreased. The strange ninjas kept up the chase and, despite their heavy equipment, did not seem to tire. "Up ahead!" shouted Sally and turned into another ruined tunnel. They scrambled over rocks and leaped over fragments of statues. Further up they could see the source of the light. The guards were lagging behind, now that they had to jump in that uncomfortable equipment. The kids ran out of the tunnel and screeched to a stop. They were at the bottom of a huge pit with smooth walls. Directly in front of them protruded a huge dragon's mouth. It was shut. "What are we gonna do?" yelled Jake. Sally ran to the top lip of the dragon and pressed a few symbols that were engraved on a tooth, not realizing that they spelled QIN SHI HUANGDI.

With a creak and a roar of falling stones, the mouth opened. Immediately they saw a crystal tube that resembled an hourglass filled with sand. The sand flowed out of a hole at the bottom. *Wait . . . Hourglass?* thought Sally. "It's a time limit!" she screamed and rushed into the open mouth. Dave and Jake followed her. The sand was almost gone as they ran down the tongue. The first guard threw his spear at them and would have killed Jake had not the sand run out. The dragon's mouth closed with a crash that resembled thunder. The spear splintered and snapped. The guards ran for the tunnel as the empty space around the dragon's head began to fill with a seemingly endless stream of sand.

Inside the dark dragon's head, Jake took out two torches and lit one. As they ran, something fell down behind them. They turned around. It was a block of slate! Then another one fell beside it. Then another one, and another one followed. Sally's eyes grew big when she saw something glowing on the wall. It was a sign: YOU WHO DEFY THE MIGHTY EMPEROR OF THE SUN AND RISING STAR SHALL BE ENTOMBED HERE FOR AS LONG AS THE SUN AND MOON SHALL RISE!

Sally cried out as more blocks fell from the ceiling. She whirled around and dashed farther into the dragon's belly. Jake and Dave hurriedly stumbled after her as the truth began to sink in. They would stay as far as possible from the falling rocks until the tunnel came to an end and then be crushed by the steadily approaching falling blocks! They reached a big chamber that had walls covered with engravings. In the center was a huge carving of a fully grown dragon engraved sideways into the wall. It was made out of gold. Sally sat down and noticed the sparkling thing that was on the dragon's neck. She ran over to it and saw that it was an amulet engraved in the throat. She pressed it, and cracks showed in the wall. Dust fell as a whole section of the wall fell down. They peered in. Suddenly Sally heard a *click* and stepped back, pushing Dave and Jake over. Just as she did, a huge sword slashed over the entrance, cutting Sally's backpack strap in two. Then there was a rumble, and something started to cover the doorway. Sally instinctively rushed in and pulled the others after her, not a moment too soon, as a wall crashed over the entrance.

Jake was about to let out his breath when an arrow flew out of a wall and thudded into the neighboring wall. Immediately another arrow came from the other side and raced toward the opposite one. "Oh, no! Not again!" groaned Jake in exhaustion as another arrow raced past. They ran to the end of the tunnel. Soon they came to a dead end. The walls and ceiling and floor were covered with designs. Sally sat down wearily and pulled out the paper they had found in the spear. *Oh! If only we had stayed there! Instead we're to be shot full of arrows!* she thought. She unfolded the yellowed script and read the poem once more. What could it mean? "Press Qin Huangdi . . . Open any door . . .' All of those useless, senseless words!" She thought. She felt a bump against her back and looked to see what it was. Oh, just another engraving, she thought, and she read it: Qin Shi Huangdi. "Listen, Mister Emperor Qin Huangdi, I wish you would stop talking in riddles!" she thought in frustration, and punched it as hard as she could. As she put her knuckles into her mouth to ease the pain, the letters began to glow, and the wall slid down into the ground. She stared at the opening and remembered the words she'd read, "Qin Huangdi . . . Open any door". . . . She smiled but decided not to tell the others of her discovery. Then she jumped in, calling to the boys. They ran and jumped in just as the arrows came too close. "Whew! How come you keep rescuing us? I didn't know damsels rescued knights instead of knights rescuing damsels!" joked Jake in relief. Then he warily went forward. They passed lots of different branches on both sides. Finally they came to a dead end. Dave frowned and said, "Let's go back and try one of those branches." First they rested and ate all the food they had left. Then they kept going.

In an hour they were kind of worried. After another hour they were very worried. And in one *more* hour they were totally terrified! Sally had twisted her ankle, so they had to make a stretcher out of a blanket and two of their walking sticks and carry her. Finally even the boys got tired. They stopped to rest. Dave noticed that they kept going higher and higher. He yawned wearily and sat on the cold tunnel floor. "We're lost in a huge maze!" he told the others in despair. Jake only nodded. Then Sally looked at the wall and saw the name QIN HUANGDI engraved on a single block of wood, along with the symbol for rest. She kicked it and was no longer surprised when that section of the wall moved up. As the boys carried her through, the wall started to come down.

Jake walked for a little while and saw daylight. He ran toward it, dragging the stretcher, until they found themselves at the bottom of another pit. In the middle of the pit was a small crystal-clear pond with fruit trees growing around it. He whooped and dragged Sally to the edge of the water. He splashed some water on her face, and she stood up. They all drank the refreshing water and ate the juicy fruits until they were full. Then Sally went to sleep, and the others did likewise.

In the morning Jake woke first. He picked up his bow and arrows and walked the perimeter of their enclosure, and something caught his eye. He had noticed sunlight on the wall! He ran over and pulled away a rotting board, revealing a window two inches wide and one foot tall. He was shocked to see that he was three hundred feet above the ground instead of in a pit! He thought about climbing out but realized that that was unrealistic. He examined the view and found himself looking at several miles' worth of destroyed buildings. The buildings were bordered by a huge castle. After a few minutes he realized that they were in a ruined tower in the castle. He was angry and scared.

He opened his mouth to yell the news to his friends, but they were sleeping. He sighed and sat down to wait. Then he noticed he had only ten more arrows left.

Suddenly he heard a bird. It sounded harsh and mocking. He looked up and saw a vulture land on top of the tower. Then another one joined it. Jake quickly pulled back the string and let go. The arrow hissed and hit the vulture in its breast. The bird choked and fell down in front of Jake. The other one tried to fly away but another arrow soon had it lying beside its twin. Jake smiled and plucked their feathers. He cut a few boughs off of the fruit trees and made fifty more arrows. He buried the leftover feathers and meat. Then he ate some fruit and drank water. Soon the others woke up.

Sally finally told the others the name that opened all the doors. Jake was angry that Sally hadn't told them sooner. Sally said he didn't need to know it before. Dave suggested exploring the small copse of trees in the middle of the enclosure. They stumbled over the undergrowth and came to a small place where there weren't any plants. The floor was made of rock and had a square hole about one yard deep that had five stones lying in pearly white sand; four were at the corners and one in the center. Suddenly Sally gasped and ran back to their camp. By the time they got there Sally had already packed some of their things. They helped her, thinking ahead. Sally grabbed the matches and her water bottle and ran into the bushes. She picked some fruit and refilled the water bottles. Then she ran farther into the bushes. Jake and Dave followed, pushing away the thorny briars. They caught up with her, only to see her jump into the pit. Jake followed, with Dave bringing up the rear. Sally stepped on the rock that had Qin Huangdi written on it, and the pit turned into a swirling sucking mass of sand! Sally was sucked in first, and Jake, too surprised to think, was pulled in also. He felt himself sliding down a narrow stone tunnel cushioned by sand. He also felt himself being thrown up and down as if by a bronco! The tunnel became narrower and narrower. It had small holes in it from erosion and felt damp. His speed decreased, and Jake felt like he was going to stop. Then the floor of the tunnel gave way, and he was falling through space!

He landed in another tunnel that was much steeper than the previous one. He thought he was going to fly off in some direction and use his head for a brake. He imagined himself morphing into a jet liner and almost laughed aloud, but the sand around his face kept him from doing so. The ride down the sand tunnel reminded him of a roller coaster. He slid faster and faster and suddenly flew out of the tunnel with a *whoosh*. He landed on a pile of sand and opened his eyes. He felt so dizzy he was afraid of throwing up. He stood up woozily and saw Sally sitting nearby, brushing herself off. He heard a muffled noise, and out of the tunnel came Dave. He lay on the sand for a while and then got up. The sand decreased and finally stopped coming at all.

Dave felt dizzy but he didn't look it. He brushed himself off and walked over to them. "Some rough slide, huh?" he said, looking a little green.

"It's a good thing we're not little kids, or we'd try it again!" said Sally, grinning. They walked over to the entrance of a hallway lit with lanterns. Jake looked at the fire and frowned. "I think someone else besides us was here!" he said, looking at the well-oiled lanterns. They walked through the hallway until they were faced with a choice. Ahead led a well-cared-for passage; to the left was a half-destroyed one. Dave lifted his hand, and they froze. An eerie chanting was coming from the tunnel ahead, becoming steadily louder. Jake leaped into the decrepit tunnel and scrambled over the debris on the floor. He jumped over a big rock and was faced with a boulder that took up the entire length of the tunnel. On top was a small space that might be big enough to squeeze through. He waited until the others caught up and explained the situation. He volunteered to go first. He tossed a rope with barbs on the end and jerked it to make sure it was safe. Looking at his friends, he took a deep breath and started up. He reached the crack and squeezed halfway through. Then he took a deep breath and wiggled until he fell to the other side. As Sally got ready to climb, the chanting got steadily closer.

"Hurry up!" whispered Dave, his face tense. "I'll go last!" Sally looked at him worriedly and started up. She got to the top and tried to get through, but her knapsack wouldn't fit. She kept trying. Suddenly the chanters marched through the tunnel and headed down the other tunnel. At that moment Sally squeezed through. As she fell, a jug dropped from her backpack and shattered on the floor. Immediately the chanters whirled. Drawing their swords, they ran at Dave. Dave gave a desperate jump but a sword chopped the rope in half. A moment later he was surrounded. The strange chanters blindfolded and gagged him and then slung him over their shoulders.

Sally jumped up and grabbed the edge of the stone. She saw Dave being hauled away and realized it was her fault that Dave was now a prisoner. She fell to the ground in shock. Jake jumped up and pulled back an arrow. Then he took it back out and lowered himself. He realized it was too risky to rescue Dave now. The chanters might kill him. He quickly scrambled back over the wall and sprinted after the priests. Sally, still numb with shock, plodded after him.

Dave hung over the smelly priest's shoulder and thought, *Well, this time I really am gonna cross the river Jordan!* The priests ran through different tunnels and passageways until Dave was dizzy. Then he heard a lock open, and he was swiftly carried through a door. The man roughly threw him down, and Dave opened his eyes. They were in a small room without chairs or benches; water pooled on the floor. The men marched out talking excitedly and shut the door behind them.. Dave sat up and tried to untie the ropes binding his wrists, but it was useless, and he knew it. He sighed and leaned against the slime-coated wall. He wondered what would happen to him now.

Jake and Sally sneaked behind the armed men who had taken Dave until they were lost in the maze of tunnels. As they walked along, Sally stepped on a stone and fell through the floor. Jake jumped to help her, but he slipped and tumbled in after her. They landed in a dark room full of garbage. They quickly headed to a side entrance and sprinted down the floor that had three inches of water. Jake saw two entrances to the side and turned into one. He ran to a rock and leaped over it. Then the tunnel turned steeply down. He glanced at his solar-powered watch and read the mini barometer. They were five thousand feet below sea level! He was shocked that the castle, which probably had hundreds of these different passageways, was still standing. He started to walk; the path turned until it was at a forty-degree slant. He suddenly had a brainstorm and pulled out his jacket. He sat on it and whizzed down! Sally saw him sledding down and sighed, pulling out her own jacket. She couldn't sit down on that! Finally she grabbed her sleeping bag and careened down after Jake. The path suddenly got even steeper, until they were headed straight down! Sally grabbed the sleeping bag from under her and got ready for a hard landing. She was surprised to see that Jake was still sitting on his jacket. She was about to call him when unexpectedly the ground evened out. Sally landed with a thump. When she caught her breath, she got back on the sleeping bag. Up ahead she could hear Jake's yells. She set her jaw and wiggled the sleeping bag until she was flying at a breakneck speed. She caught up with Jake and slowed down a bit. Suddenly she couldn't feel the ground any more. She whipped the bag from under her feet just as they hit something with a thump. She heard Jake land beside her, and they sat up.

"We're in a boat!" exclaimed Jake. They heard yells behind them and looked back. Then they started laughing. The strange men had been preparing to go out in the boat, and they had landed just as the men had untied it! The strong current quickly pulled them to the center and twirled them about like a matchstick. They had to duck, as arrows flew at them and landed all around the boat. Suddenly they heard an excited murmur from the men behind them and sat up just in time to see a flaming arrow fly overhead. They followed it with their eyes. Suddenly it exploded in a burst of fire, smoke, and sparks. Jake suddenly remembered that the Chinese had invented gunpowder and realized they were probably shooting the exploding arrows in order to sink the boat! He grabbed a board and deflected another arrow. Then he felt the boat shudder. He looked over the side and saw that they were about to hit a stretch of rapids. He braced himself as he boat hit the first foaming stretch. The water fairly boiled as it rushed over rocks. In some places it disappeared into deep holes in the middle of the river and nearly caught the boat in its deadly jaws. They held on tightly when the boat hit several rocks and shook as if it would burst and send them into the merciless river. Then Jake was struck with a pang of fear. Up ahead the water disappeared into an abyss of the deep, dark underground. But Jake saw something that gave him a glimmer of hope. Right on the edge of the river where the river slid under the second layer of rock and disappeared into the huge hole was a huge boulder that they could use as a ramp to fly to the second layer. Franicaly Jake grabbed the rifle and pushed against the rocks to get enough momentum but there was no need. The current carried them forward with breakneck speed and they hit the rock with such force that the boat was split in half and both of them flew to the second layer. Jake landed safely on his knees but as he looked around he saw to his horror Sally crashing against the edge and plunging down! "No!" he screamed and thrust the rifle at her. She grabbed it and hand by hand Jake reached her arms and pulled her onto the ledge. Fifteen seconds later a crash sounded at the bottom. "The boat . . ." whispered Jake. Sally trembled but then crawled to the edge and looked down. "That could have been us!" she said in awe. Jake nodded and stood up, shakily helping Sally too. But she made it on her own and leaned against the wall. "We better go!" yelled Jake as the ledge creaked and tilted. Sally threw back her hair and ran to the opposite wall. Jake walked over to Sally and pointed to the entrance in the wall. They walked through the arch and disappeared in the darkness.

As they walked along, Jake thought about what to do. He imagined what he would have thought if someone had told him that one day he would end up here, hundreds of feet underground. He smiled, imagining himself laughing at that person. Then the smile vanished from his face as he remembered Dave. How was he? *Where* was he? These worrying questions crowded his mind. He remembered how many times Dave had saved them and wondered if he would ever see him again. Suddenly he heard Sally scream. As he turned to ask her what was the matter, he felt the ground give way. He reached and grasped Sally's hand as they flew down a curving tunnel. Then the tunnel turned straight down before it ended and threw them out. Immediately the entrance was sealed off. Jake looked around and saw that they were in a perfectly round chamber made of six-sided blocks. He saw the words QIN SHI HUANGDI almost immediately. He pressed it, expecting it to open, but nothing happened. He pressed the blue symbol again, but it remained firm. Jake was surprised, then frightened. If QIN SHI HUANGDI didn't open anything, what did? Then he noticed that most of the blocks had QIN SHI HUANGDI on them. He ran around, frantically pressing. As he pressed a yellow one, it dropped through. He whirled to show it to Sally and saw her jump into a huge hole that had opened in the middle of the floor. As he jumped in after her, he saw the lever stop and come back down. He jumped in at the last second and felt the air tremble from the force of the fall.

As he fell on the floor he saw something mysterious glowing on the walls, ceiling, and floor. He touched it but it was hard. He looked around and saw Sally. She looked eerie in the weird light. She walked over, looking frightened. "Look what the glowing words say!" she whispered. He read them; they all said QIN SHI HUANGDI. He pushed them, but they didn't budge an inch. In the strange light from the emperor's name, they walked softly and solemnly down the well-lit passageway past different carvings on the wall. Then they saw a door on the left. A sign over it said KITCHEN. Soon they passed another on the right. This one said BEDROOM. They passed more tunnels with other signs: WELL, TOWER, TEMPLE, GUARD HOUSE, and many others. Jake pointed at one that said LIONS PIT. "Like the one Daniel was in!" laughed Jake. When they passed one saying THRONE ROOM they decided to walk down it for a bit. They soon reached total darkness, and Jake lit a candle he kept in his backpack for emergencies. Soon they reached a dead end. On the floor was an elaborate carving of a dragon's face. From its mouth protruded a chain. Jake pulled on the chain, and the head came up.

Suddenly below them they could see the emperor himself. Jake held his breath. Suddenly he saw Uncle Lou, bound in chains, before the emperor. The emperor stretched out his sword and said in a voice resembling thunder, "Tonight you shall be thrown to the dragon! And that stranger will be too!" The guards grabbed Lou and dragged him away. Sally and Jake looked at each other and quietly closed the lid. They ran back to the main tunnel to discus what had happened. Jake sat down next to the door labeled KITCHEN. He sighed as his tummy rumbled. "I just wish we could eat something hot!" he said wistfully. Sally nodded. Then Jake said, "Hey! The door labeled throne room led to the throne room, so why shouldn't this one lead to the kitchen?"

Sally's eyes widened. "Good idea—let's try it!" she said, getting up. Jake also scrambled up, and they were soon jogging down the hall to the end. Jake lifted the now-familiar head carefully and peeked out. They were right by the ventilation shaft, and from below rose a heavenly smell. Jake looked down, and his mouth watered. Right below them was a huge turkey roasting on a fire, with all sorts of sauces and seasonings. As he watched a man, obviously the head chef, took a jug from a shelf and poured some of its speckled reddish brown contents over the bird. Then he took a long, thin spear made of polished silver and poked the bird in several places. He plucked two bottles from his waist and sprinkled their contents over a dish that resembled rice and a meaty mush with pepper all over it. Then he barked an order, and two sparkling clean attendants grabbed the iron rod that held the turkey and flipped it. They grabbed the salad and dumped it carefully on a huge golden plate and covered it with oil. Then they grabbed the turkey and put it on top of the salad and stuffed it with a strange mixture of potatoes, some sort of fish meat, and a brown mush that resembled chili but didn't smell like it.

Jake almost fell down when the attendants brought a huge castle carved out of various fruits, a bunch of different salads, some sort of meat that resembled poop, and a huge plate of sushi. Jake was staring down at the food and felt they just had to get some. He watched as the cooks brought in all sorts of golden, silver, and crystal pitchers full of all sorts of liquids. In the crystal ones he saw a red wine, a purple wine, a white wine, and another one full of something bubbling. Then the chefs sprayed the air around the food with something and walked out of the kitchen. The temptation was too much to resist, and Jake leaped down. He helped Sally to the floor, and they armed themselves with a bunch of golden and crystal utensils Jake found on a shelf. They started devouring the food. When they had finished Jake had an idea. He and Sally picked the half-eaten chicken and pushed it up into the entrance. Then they also transported all the wines, salads, and desserts.

Just as they climbed back into the entryway, the door opened and the chefs entered. For a moment there was a stunned silence. Then the chef started screaming and picked up a big spoon, hitting a particularly frightened boy. From what the kids could understand of the chef's hysterical screaming, the boy was an orphan and had been enslaved by the mean chef. The chef threw the spoon in a corner and smashed the boy's face with his meaty fist. The boy flew across the room, his nose and lips a fountain of blood. At that sight, Sally exploded. She laid the big chef out with a drop kick and finished him off with a blow to his temple. The heavy man went out like a light. Then she turned a flip and with a yell flicked her feet at two guards. Her blows landed on their necks, and they started to fall woozily to the floor. As they fell, Sally smashed their heads together. She saw a cupboard and whipped it open; she saw that it was full of pots, pans, dishes, and glasses. She grinned and sent them all flying across the room. Then she grabbed a stack of plates and flung them like heavy Frisbees at the remaining guards.

Meanwhile, Jake bathed the unconscious boy's head with wine, because they didn't have any water. He stopped the bleeding and gave him a drink of the bubbly stuff. The boy's eyes fluttered, and he lifted his head. He jumped back in fright at the sight of unfamiliar faces and the unconscious men on the floor.

"W-who are you?" he asked in rapid Chinese. Jake grinned and introduced himself and Sally. The boy felt better after another sip of the sparkly stuff but still didn't trust the foreigners entirely. Finally they had to show him the secret entrance and tell him the whole story. The boy laughed when they came to the part about Sally smashing the head chef. He told them that his name was Chang Lang and not "fly-brained goat," as the chef had called him. He also said that he was fourteen years old. He was born in the month of the dragon, which was supposed to make him lucky, but so far his life had been miserable. He listened to the story about Dave and said he knew where the pit was. "It's a horrible place!" he said with a shudder.

Suddenly they heard yells. The boy's face paled. "It's Black Bamboo, the chief of the guards!" he said, frightened. "No one has ever escaped from him yet!"

Sally laughed and said. "Look at this!" Chang stared at the last rifle. "What? It's just a stick!" Sally pointed the rifle at a lantern and fired. Chang laughed and exclaimed. "I like it! We have big sound too!" Sally looked doubtful. "You mean you've heard this kind of thing before?" she asked.

"Ah!" said Chang, laughing, "Many, many, times I have witnessed the dragon powder destroy metal and even rocks!" He wore a secretive look and pulled a small bag out of his pocket. "If you put fire on this, it will make a big bang and lots of fire and smoke!"

Sally opened the bag and looked at the silvery gray dust and laughed. "Nice try, but I'm afraid ash doesn't explode!"

Chang laughed too. "Ah, but this isn't ash! It's dragon powder!" Then he motioned for silence. The teens grew quiet and listened to the screaming and moaning that had resumed in the kitchen. Suddenly Chang raced to the secret entrance with a devilish look. Sally and Jake looked at each other and shrugged. Then Chang ran back, grabbed them by the collars, and dragged them down the hall. They had barely gone ten feet when the air exploded in a bang. Smoke entered the hallway, and they heard an agonizing scream coming from the kitchen. Chang grinned and sneaked toward the kitchen. What Sally saw astonished her. The kitchen was black, and two of the walls had been destroyed by the blast. Black Bamboo was lying on the ground, unconscious, while the head cook was protruding from the wall. Suddenly the door was smashed to pieces and a man, who Chang identified as Diaz Drano, rushed in with a drawn sword.

As Sally tried to back up the duct, she slipped, and her head stuck from the pipe in plain view of all the soldiers. Luckily, none of them noticed her, but as she pulled herself up, Black Bamboo's eyes fluttered and he saw her. As he opened his mouth to shout, he reached for his razor-sharp sword. Sally was clearly his target.

龙4 THE GREAT WALL

At that moment Sally heard a barely audible *whisk,* and a good-sized rock conked Black Bamboo on the head. Sally looked up and saw Chang looking at Black Bamboo with hate in his eyes. The other soldiers did not seem to notice what happened, so the teens quietly sneaked back to the main hallway. "Whew! That was close!" said Sally in relief.

"I'll say!" agreed Jake as he wiped his brow.

Chang smiled and said, "You're welcome!"

Sally gaped at him. "You mean . . . !"

Chang grinned. "Yep. I was the one who knocked his brains loose."

Sally smiled, but then a worried look crossed her face, and she said, "Well, I guess we should rescue Dave. I mean, here we are, eating and talking our heads off while Dave is probably freezing in a cold dungeon!"

"Sufferin' snakes! I forgot about him!" gasped Jake.

Chang yawned and said, "Fine. Follow me."

An hour later the three of them were crawling down a cold, gray stone tunnel. "Are you sure this is the right way? I don't mean to be a sop, but after the first three tunnels . . ." Sally grimaced as the cold seeped through her.

Chang sighed and suddenly stopped. "Okay. I think the trapdoor is just about heeeeeeeeeeeeere!" he yelled as he crashed through the ancient wooden door. Soon the trio was sitting in a dark corner, soothing their bruises. "Ugh! That was one way of getting to Dave quick!"

"Hey don't blame me! How was I supposed to know that the wood was that rotten?" growled Chang.

Sally rolled her eyes. "Okay. Yeah, Yeah! So are we gonna just sit here or what!" she said as she scanned the dark dungeon corridor. "This place is kinda damp you know!"

"Yeah! And kinda musty too!" grinned Jake, imitating his sister. Then they heard a creaking noise. Down the hallway a cell opened, and two men dragged out a gaunt, dirty figure.

"Come on! The dragon sacrifice must not wait!" barked one of the guards. Then Sally gasped. The figure was Dave! As the guards went down the dreary tunnel, the three friends silently crept after them.

It had been a long, tiresome day for Dave. He had been pre-interrogated, interrogated, and re-interrogated, and now he was being hauled off to be a sacrifice? He groaned and tried to speed up when one of the guards prodded him with his spear butt. They walked up a long flight of steps and came out of a heavily guarded door. Dave looked around and saw that he was in a crowded marketplace. The mob was chanting, "*Si-lang*! Si-lang! Death! Death! Death!"

Dave sneered back at them. "Right! Sing long! And may your voices burst!"

In the center was a large block of stone. The guards dragged him toward it. Suddenly Dave was face to face with a dragon. Its mouth was wide open, and Dave saw white and green flames inside. Smoke came pouring out of the monster's nostrils, and its eyes glittered. Then a trumpet blared out, and a regal-looking man came out of a huge, gold-plated double door in the center of the marketplace. A small, wizened old man followed the tall man. He carried a wicked sword; its blade was made of diamond. The moonlight shone on the razor-sharp sword, which caused it to glow a bluish white color. Then the door opened once more, and a man wearing a dragon suit came out. The suit was black, with tiny red and gold dragons on it, and was about five sizes too big. As the man stumbled forward, he tripped and fell flat on his face. The crowd roared. Dave looked at him and realized that he was the executioner. As the regal man started to read a long speech, Dave hung his head. There was no way to avoid it. Tonight he would die.

Back in the castle, Chang stopped at the great gates that were swarming with guards and then ran back into the tunnel. "Back!" he whispered. "Back! There's a pile of guards at the entrance!" After fifteen minutes of wandering and another twenty of climbing, they had a rope tied to a tree on the mountainside. Jake stood on top of a tower holding the other end.

Meanwhile, in the market, the speech was finished. Amid chanting and yelling, the small wizened man lifted up the gleaming sword with trembling hands, about to pierce Dave through the chest. The executioner readied himself to lift up Dave's body and hurl it into the fiery oven. Suddenly Jake swooped down! He grabbed Dave in one hand and kicked the executioner, who was Black Bamboo, into the fiery mouth instead. But the wily man was tough; with one hand he pushed off from the fiery interior and crumpled to the ground from the shock. His right hand was entirely burned off.

Dave grabbed the fallen sword. Jake grabbed him, and in another instant they were swept away.. Jake swung high, high up on the mountain and dropped onto a ledge, pulling Dave after him. At the same moment, Sally, higher up on the mountain, pushed a large boulder down the mountainside, causing an avalanche that barely missed the two refugees. After a quick warm huddle they raced higher up the mountain, toward the Great Wall of China.

As they climbed, Chang told them that the Great Wall was only ten miles away. All they had to do was to climb this huge mountain and get down the other side. Finally, after a long, grueling climb, they reached the top. The view was spectacular. On a nearby mountain they could see a long, yellowish gray line. It was the Great Wall of China! Sally, Jake, and Dave gaped at the beauty. Then out of the mist they heard

Chang yell, "C'mon! Help me pull this wing up!" The trio whirled around and saw Chang pulling a broken piece of a plane wing.

"Hey! Where did you get that?" yelled Jake.

Chang laughed. "I found it! An old plane must have crashed on this slope." Sally shrugged and started to tug at the old piece of metal.

"Why isn't it rusty?" asked Jake as he tugged at the heavy wing.

"Because it's made of aluminum, and aluminum doesn't rust. Like you. You're like a rubber ball! No matter how many times you get hit you bounce back up!" she joked.

Jake looked as if he were on the brink of desperation. "What kind of crazy joke is that? I have no idea what you're talking about! Me, snacks, vegetables, wings, aluminum . . . That is the most absorbed thing I ever heard of!"

Sally giggled. "It's *absurd*, not *absorbed*. There is no such thing as absorbed!"

Carrying the wing, they reached an icy strip of snow. "All aboooooooooard!" yelled Jake, imitating a train conductor. The kids jumped onto the piece of thin aluminum and held on tight. Slowly at first, but then with more and more speed, the makeshift sled hurtled down the mountainside. The wing hit bumps and spun until the teens couldn't see straight. Then they hit a huge snowdrift and sailed into the air over a huge crack in the mountainside! As the wing spun, Sally felt the pull harder than the others did. She shot off the wing and seemed to plunge into the abyss. But as she fell, she grasped the edge of the wing. As soon as they crossed over the crevasse, Sally tried to climb back up, but her strength failed her. She fell toward the hard, icy bottom.

The wing hit an ancient log hidden in the snow and dislodged it. The log followed the wing down the slope, first slowly, but then it overtook the wing. As Sally fell toward the log, she had no hope of surviving the crash. When she opened her eyes, she wondered why she wasn't feeling a million breaks in her bones. The ground was flying past at a blur, and she realized that she was on a huge log with a three-foot diameter. She sat up and clung to a stubby branch to keep from flying off the monster tree.

She clung to the tree trunk. Soon the log arrived at a huge overhang and sailed over an even wider crevice than the first. Sally's eyes flew wide open. Then she heard a sickening crunch. The trunk stopped, with one end resting on a tall iceberg in the middle of the crevice and the other end wedged into a crack on top of the broad prickly second end and the trunk scraped on the rough broken ice. The trunk swayed, barely remaining aloft, it seemed, though it was actually quite safe. The ice below towered into a skyscraper whose edge stuck through the middle of the trunk. Sally heard the heavy wing approaching and quickly crawled to the very edge of the log. Just as she grabbed the edge, the wing hit the edge and soared right next to her! Timing it perfectly, she leaped and landed on the wing. Jake looked surprised and happy, and Chang looked pretty relieved, but Dave, as usual, was still worried. *Probably wondering if I broke any arms or legs!* Sally thought, and she smiled.

The wing bounced off the log and hit the opposite bank in an explosion of ice and snow. Soon their makeshift sled reached the bottom. As they neared the Great Wall, one side of the wing hit a tree trunk. The wing became a blur of spinning metal and flung the friends into the snow. The foursome gazed in awe at the huge monument before them. "How will we ever get up this wall?" asked Sally, as she gazed at the top.

Jake tried to sling a rope and hook on the top, but it was too high, and the wind kept blowing the rope away. He shrugged and sat on a rock. "It's too high!" he said, and he took a biscuit out of his ration pack. Then Dave whispered something into Chang's ear.

Chang looked puzzled and said "No. Why?" Dave whispered again, and Chang's face lit up. "Okay!" he said and headed toward a pair of trees standing side by side. They were young and only twenty feet tall. Chang climbed up and tied one end of a rope to the top of one tree and the other to its neighbor. Then he scrambled down and cut the rope.

Then Dave called Sally and Jake and motioned them to help him and Chang bend the trees. As they hauled he explained. "We're going to tie one end of the rope to a rock and catapult it over the wall! We added some hooks." Jake looked blank but Sally got the idea.

"So we're gonna use the trees because their pull is stronger, right?" she asked smiling.

"Right!" answered Dave. He grinned as the trees groaned. When they were sure they couldn't pull them any more, Dave put the rock into the pouch in the center of the rope. Then they heaved the rope one more time and let go. The rock flew over the wall and hit something solid with a *clang*. The four of them slapped hands and started to climb up the rope.

As Jake got over the wall, he saw a soldier come out of a tower not too far away. He headed toward Jake but didn't see him. Jake hid in a pile of shields and held his breath. The burly guard was carrying a spear. He approached Jake's hiding place. Suddenly the guard glanced at the pile of weapons and noticed Jake's foot. He frowned and went over to investigate. As he saw Jake, he opened his mouth to yell, but Jake grabbed the spear and smashed the guard in the forehead with the butt end. Then he called to Sally and Dave. When all of them were on top of the wall, Chang guided them to a window. He went through first and was met by a fearsome-looking man with a patch over one eye and a rusty cutlass in his hand. Chang smashed the man with a blow on his face and received a cut on the arm as the guard stumbled backward. Chang wrenched the cutlass away and ran the man through. "My motto is 'Take no prisoners and you will live long'!" he said as he wiped the blade clean on the dead man's clothes.

Sally looked a little green when she saw the bloodstained floor. "Ugh! Look at all the blood!" She gasped a little and stumbled to the door. There she saw a bow and a quiver of arrows. She picked it up and slung it over her shoulder. "Let's get outta here!" she said and went out the door. Jake, Dave, and Chang searched the room for weapons and found three very nice swords and five daggers. They took these for themselves and, smiling, stepped outside.

"Where's Sally?" asked Jake. Chang looked around and pushed Dave to the floor. An arrow flew overhead and stuck into the wooden door. Chang took out his two daggers and grabbed Jake's and Dave's daggers too. He hurled them at the small army that stood before them, and then he yanked out a purple bag. He lit a short fuse and, putting it on the floor, jumped into the room they had just left, dragging his two friends behind him. He closed and bolted the door. "Cover your ears!" he warned. A second later a huge explosion rocked the tower. The door blasted inward, and a cloud of smoke came in. At that moment Jake noticed a symbol in a block on the floor. It was the emperor's name! His eyes clouded as the smoke crushed them, and he slammed his foot down on the sign. Nothing happened. Then he pulled and jumped on it, but nothing seemed to work. Then Dave had an inspiration. As the roof swayed, he pushed the block aside and revealed a set of stairs. He and the two other boys hurtled down into the dark hallway and slammed the lid shut behind them. Then the world turned dark.

When they woke up they couldn't see anything. Jake rummaged in his backpack until he found a torch. He sighed and lit it. The torch burst into flames. They headed down the slimy passageway until they came to a wooden door with a rusty lock on it. They were able to smash through the rotten wood with their swords. They stepped into an underground hallway. On the walls were burning torches; there were twenty doors on the right side and five on the left. On the end was a huge set of double doors. The three boys crept over to the huge doors and their eyes almost bugged out. The doors were solid gold, imbedded with assorted diamonds, emeralds, rubies, and other precious minerals. The doors were locked, but Jake took out the ancient samurai sword he had carried all the way from home and swung it at the lock. The bronze shrieked in protest as the finely honed blade ripped through it. Jake threw the lock into a corner and heaved at the heavy doors. Silently they opened. "Well oiled!" he noted. Chang nodded and helped him pull. When the door was fully open, they looked inside and gasped at the huge room inside. In the front was a gigantic throne surrounded by a lot of smaller ones. The rest of the room was filled with elaborate chairs made from golden oak and covered with silver. The smaller chairs were divided in groups of five, and each group was set around a small table, with a silver plate and a silver cup at each chair. On each side of the huge hall was a large door. Behind the throne was another smaller door shaped like a dragon's mouth. The three boys walked over to the heavily embroidered door and looked at the panel in the middle. It was a sort of puzzle. Jake looked at each little square and then at the one empty space. He moved the squares around and created a little symbol for water.

"Hey! That's neat! It's like a Rubik's cube!" exclaimed Dave. "Let me have a try!" Soon the boys were playing with the little lock like it was a toy. Then, quite by accident, Jake made the symbol QIN. Then it finally hit him. "We need to spell Qin Huangdi!" he shouted excitedly, and he quickly moved the little squares. As soon as the last square was in place, the door opened to reveal a large piece of parchment instead. On the parchment was a message. It said:

> Greetings my son! For only one of mine could solve this riddle!
>
> I see you are also an adventurer, for no one else would have tried to fulfill this quest. Truly I was called the wise one, and I have concealed this treasure with many traps that only a descendant of mine could figure out. If you choose to go on with this quest, then I bid you good luck! Be mindful of the many dangers in here, and remember, there is no turning back. The lights will be activated as the parchment falls down. Farewell, my son!
>
> Qin Shi Huangdi, your emperor.

"What does he mean, 'No turning back'? We could always just open this door and walk out!" exclaimed Jake.

Chang looked unsure. "You and Dave may think so, but we had quite a few trickeries at the old ruins, and let me tell you, they were not pleasant!" he said doubtfully. Jake shrugged and slashed through the parchment. Immediately it fell to the ground, and behind it a dozen lanterns lit up. The three boys entered the round room, and immediately the door closed behind them and blended into the wall. Only then did Jake understand the words "No turning back."

"We're trapped! Either we succeed and get to the treasure and the exit, or we *don't* get to the treasure *or* to the exit! I'm pretty sure the exit is near the treasure," he explained.

Dave felt nervous but wore a calm face. "Okay, guys. These lanterns will burn out sooner or later, so we'd best get going," he said, trying not to panic. He walked over to the opposite wall. There were three doors, and on each was a rhyme. The first one went like this:

> Follow me and you will find,
> More treasures than the world's combined!
> But make sure your guide is true,
> Or else you'll never see the sky, so blue! 电光 (lightning)

The second read,

> Right here you'll find both peace and rest!
> And if the treasure is your quest,
> You'll reach it with no elaborate traps,
> But slow and steady, with a map! 龟 (turtle)

And the last one said, rabbit
> Quickly will your way go through,
> Not too many dangers, too!

Bonuses you'll not receive,
Qin will never be deceived!

Dave stared at Jake when he finished.

"What do those little pictures mean?" asked Jake.

Dave shrugged and inspected them. "You know, this reminds me of the little proverb about the race between the rabbit and the turtle!" he said, grinning wryly.

Jake sighed and said, "Yeah, I remember! 'Slow and steady wins the race', huh?" He walked over to the second door. "Slow and steady . . . I wonder if . . ." He turned around and shouted, "I've got it! If we take the second door it will take us longer to reach the goal! If we take the third one, we will pass through the maze quickly, but there will be more traps than in the second one! And since the first one says we'll have an extra bonus but it will have tons of traps, the lightning must mean that it's the most dangerous choice!" he concluded triumphantly.

Dave looked puzzled, but then he got it. "Oh! So now the question is, which one do we take?" he said, and he sat onto the cold stone floor. As Chang began to walk over to his two friends, he felt something hot drip onto his back. He turned around and saw the wax picture of a crown behind the torch melt, revealing a message behind it. HURRY, OH, MY SON! FOR THE TORCHES SHALL TURN TO ASHES IN A HUNDRED HEARTBEATS! HASTEN AND CHOOSE! Chang broke out in cold sweat. "Hurry up, guys ! We have about a minute until these torches burn up!' he yelled.

Dave grasped up the situation at once. "Let's choose the first one! I'd like to get out of here as fast as possible, and danger must also mean faster!" he said quickly, and he shut the opened dragon's mouth mounted on the first door. The door, almost a foot thick, slowly rolled up. The three boys ran through and rushed into another room, which was still dark. Finally as the door finally rolled as high as it could go, something snapped, and the whole structure came down. *Crash!* went the door, and instantly the room was lit by ten torches.

The boys were in an even larger room that had ten doors in it. Each one was identical to the other, and in front of each one was a soldier. Jake wasn't bothered, since the soldiers were made of stone, but as he headed toward them he saw them start to move forward. He gasped. Crying out in alarm, he whipped out his sword and met the first one head on! He smashed the long saber from the cold stone fingers and dealt it a blow that sent the head rolling. He smashed another in half and saw Dave karate kick one over. Soon the remaining soldiers had reached the center. Suddenly, as they crashed into one another, the center opened up, and the remains of the soldiers fell through.

Then a beautiful war chariot rose up. It revolved and started to sink back down. As the boys leaped at it, the ten doors opened, and hundreds of soldiers came out, each moving on still legs toward the center as if on a roller. As the boys landed in the bottom of the chariot, the center snapped shut and the chariot hit the something solid. The room was flooded with light, and the boys found themselves in a room covered with tripwires. Jake took out a small razor-sharp dagger and cut through one of the lines. Immediately an ax dropped out of the ceiling and, missing Jake by an inch, cut the dagger blade in half. Jake stared at the other half of the dagger and at the floor into which the ax had disappeared. He had an idea. After cutting the next line, he quickly placed his sword under it. A boulder came down. It deflected off the thin, sharp blade, crashed into a bunch of other wires, and set off a bunch of traps at once.

The three boys hid in the bottom of the chariot until the dust settled. Only one line remained. Jake cut it, and a large piece of silk fluttered down. The message written on it said: WELL DONE! ENTER YOUR PRIZE! A shining door appeared in the wall. But Jake was suspicious. He took his bow and tied a piece of paper to an arrow. Then he shot it at the shining door. As the arrow crossed the threshold, a sword chopped it in half, and a muffled boom was heard. Then a cloud of smoke rolled in. As it cleared it revealed the wrecked door and debris all over the floor. The three boys got out of the chariot and started to gather up their things. Jake noticed a small box in the front of the chariot. He pried it open with his sword and saw a ring inside. He put it on and stepped into the darkness after his friends.

They were in a small corridor with a brightly lit room at the end. There were ten suits of youth's clothes and three of maiden's clothes, evidently royal clothes. The silk suits were embroidered with gold, silver, and gems. There were royal shoes, turbans, and a bag of gold for each suit. For the boys there were spears, huge axes, swords, and shields. There was also a beautiful bow and a quiver full of diamond-tipped arrows on the floor. Jake took a sword and shield, while Dave took a battle ax. Chang chose a shield and a spear. After they had all dressed in the new clothes and taken a spare pair, he took two pairs of ladies clothes and the bow, along with the full quiver. They stepped out and found themselves staring at the throne. They ran through the hall and crashed through the huge double doors. They rushed upstairs and smashed through the rubble. As Jake came out, he saw Sally on the top of the wall, a huge man swinging a sword at her.

Sally waited for the sword to pierce her, but it never did. Its owner fell to the ground, transfixed by an arrow in his heart. Suddenly a beautifully robed figure flew at her from the wall below with a sword in his hands. He landed on the tower top and, grabbing her, leaped off the roof. She screamed, but then she recognized the brown face. It was Jake! He landed lightly on the wall and set her down. Moments later two more figures, as nicely dressed as Jake, sneaked out of the shadows. Then all four friends started running up the wall to the top of the mountain.

As they reached the top they were greeted by a fearsome sight. Charging at them was a horde of warriors. They tried to turn back, but even more soldiers were coming at them from the other side. Jake looked at the pile of weapons lying by a second tower and grabbed a large, yellow circular shield. "C'mon!" he yelled and handed it to Chang. Chang looked puzzled but took the shield. Then Jake handed Dave a red, square shield and Sally a badge-shaped one. Then he grabbed a long oval one for himself and, after snatching a sturdy spear, leaped off the wall. The others stared at each other in bewilderment, but seeing as there was no choice, they followed him. The first arrow hissed past. Dave grabbed an extra shield and leaped off; three arrows struck his extra shield. As the four friends coasted on their little sled shields, it hailed arrows. Quickly they tossed away their new weapons to make their sleds lighter. As they slid out of arrow range, a large rock landed just behind Jake's sled, covering him with snow. Sally looked back and saw a catapult flinging boulders at them.

Just as they seemed out of the catapult's range, a huge boulder smashed into Dave's sled, sending him flying into the air. *I'm glad I have a second shield with me!* he thought as he landed and slowed down. Arrows struck the shield and broke off. But as he picked up speed, he looked ahead and saw the other three far ahead of him. He looked for a way to go faster and spotted a strip of ice. He maneuvered the shield over to it and felt his sled speed up. "Wow! This is really moving!" he shouted in exhilaration as the sled rocketed down the slope. Soon he had passed his friends and pulled at least fifty feet ahead of them. He waved as he passed them and was still smiling when he hit a rough patch. The sled bucked and spun like a wild horse, and Dave could barely hold on. He gasped in relief as the turbulence eased off. Then he heard excited shouts behind him. He looked back and groaned. The rest of the gang was having the time of their young lives as the sleds did their best to pitch their unwanted cargo off.

Then he heard a roaring noise far ahead. He squinted against the flying snow and screamed in horror. Not a hundred yards ahead was a huge cliff. Dave turned to warn his friends, but it was too late. He shot off the edge and sailed into the snow-encrusted air. The wind shrieked and howled as it roared over hundreds of feet of icy, snowy ground. As Dave looked down he saw the ground rushing up to meet him. He closed his eyes and gripped the edge of the shield. In quick succession four different sleds smashed against the steep, snowy slope and hurtled on down the mountain. When Dave landed, he felt the air whoosh out of his lungs. He grunted and, gritting his teeth, held on tightly. The sled reached two hundred miles per hour! The three others scrunched up and fought to breathe, since their lungs were not as developed as Dave's. Finally they reached the bottom and hurtled into space once more.

In the large village below, people could see four shapes flying through the air, crashing through the roof of the Buddhist monk's hut. The owner leaped up. "Ai caramba! Vat is you doing here?" he exclaimed as the senseless bodies fell to the floor. The lady of the house, a plump Puerto Rican, hustled into the room and quickly took charge. She barked an order at her reluctant husband and grabbed Jake and Dave. The thin man picked up the other two adventurers and laid them out on a couch. As the snow on their clothes melted, the couple noticed that three of their guests were dressed very richly. The man stared at the treasure, and his hands itched to grab some of it. As soon as his wife left the room, he started to yank the bracelet from Chang's arm. At that moment Jake came to. He saw the man remove the bracelet and put it on the floor. As the man reached for a second bracelet, Jake leaped up and, yanking his sword out, placed it under the man's throat.

"Let go or die!" he said. The man shuddered in surprise.

The man slowly turned around and said, "Why, monsieur! Surely I deserve something for taking care of you! Besides, who is to stop me?" he asked, grabbing a spear off the wall.

Jake smiled grimly and answered, "By the order of Qin Shi Huangdi the Great! May fortune smile on him, and may he live in peace!"

Faeroe, the monk, first looked astonished, and then he laughed. "Hah! Who'd ya say? Qin? Za emperor? I am afraid Qin died a long time ago!" he said nastily.

By then the remaining three had woken up and drawn their blades. "True!" said Jake.

Then Dave spoke up. "But his warriors live on!"

The man stood up and looked around uneasily. "And who are you?" he asked.

Sally smiled and answered, "We're his friends!"

Faeroe turned red and quickly backed out of the room. "Maria! Our guests have voken up!" he shouted. Soon the woman came in with four bowls and a large pot of soup. She divided it up and handed out bread too. Soon Sally, who had taken a course on Spanish in school, was having a fairly pleasant conversation with the mistress. When they finished eating, the boys put on their usual clothes and hung the Chinese garments in front of the fireplace to dry. Then they went outside and fixed the thatched roof with tar. The next day when it was time to leave, Jake opened a small velvet bag and took out a gold coin. He gave it to Maria and bid her good-bye. They packed up their fancy clothes and put on their old threadbare ones. "Adios!" shouted Sally as they crossed the street and disappeared among the snow-covered houses.

As they walked along the snowy street, Jake stopped at a *tourista* shop and bought a snowboard. Sally looked around and bought a pair of collapsible skis, claiming that they had more style. Dave bought a snowboard called the Snowsurfer. It was like an extra long snowboard, with a sail attached to a long pole in the center. Chang got a Snow Slicker sled that had metal runners and a windshield. It could even turn! They left the shop happy and trekked to the supply store by the train station, a mile or two away. Jake bought four snowmobiles with their gold and filled them up with diesel, which in the mountains cost ten sixty-five a gallon. He bought four snowsuits, four pairs of boots, Snow Barrier visors, one hundred packets of hot cocoa, a pot, some sugar and salt, and four pairs of thermal gloves. He also bought four plastic canisters, each holding twelve gallons of diesel, and six rucksacks of supplies. He also bought four helmets with built-in mikes and four handheld, solar radios with fifty-hour batteries. "Come on! Let's get these tin cans rollin'!" he shouted and started his engine. *Prrrr* went the huge snow machine as it backfired and then shot over the snow. "Oh, yeah! Let's see how much snow this baby can kick up!" he yelled as the steady roar of the engine increased. He slowly pushed the pedal to the floor. *Tsssssssh!* shrieked the engine as the machine kicked up the snow into a huge wall and reached one-hundred eighty miles per hour.

Sally clenched her teeth and growled through the headset, "Okay! Let's see what you can do! Here's the deal. I put the pedal to the metal, and you give it all you have!" She pushed the pedal down as far as it could go and released the brake. *Krrrowr!* boomed the engine as the snowmobile reared up and leaped down Jake's path, where it finally put its nose back down. The silver and pink colored motorsled shot behind Jake's, slowly gaining ground as the speedometer reached two-hundred miles per hour. Dave followed, and then Chang. Sally slowed down and ended up last. Jake's snowmobile had the hardest time because it was at the front and had to blaze the trail.

As the four machines struggled through the deep drifts, Sally heard faint popping sounds and saw little spurts of snow exploding around her and her friends. She looked back and almost fell off of her snowmobile at what she saw. Behind her were three black snowmobiles, and on each one sat two black figures, one driving and other shooting a machine gun. Sally pulled out her pistol and fired several times at the pursuing snowmobiles. The first one exploded, sending its passengers high into the air. As the other two were being left behind, two more snowmobiles appeared in front. Jake fired back, but he soon felt a bullet graze his cheek. Dave heard a steadily roaring sound, growing louder by the second. He looked into the distance and saw a small speck that turned into a helicopter. They were outnumbered, outgunned, and outmaneuvered! As the first two snowmobiles exploded, Dave saw one of the men leap off and hide behind a boulder. Suddenly a fierce burst of gunfire sounded, and Jake felt the snowmobile shudder. The bullets had pierced the snowmobile clean through!

龙5 LOST IN THE MOUNTAINS

"Oof!" grunted Jake as the snowmobile's engine sputtered. He looked up at the helicopter and then back at his friends. Then he saw something that gave him an idea. The man with the gun was sitting under a snow bank! Jake carefully took aim and fired at the snow bank. It collapsed and covered the man. Quickly the four mobiles raced past the pile of snow and roared behind a huge tree. Now Dave who was first raced into the mountains and shot through a narrow crevice. He raced down the crevice and waited until the others managed to squeeze in. Jake was last with a badly smoking snowmobile. He grounded to a halt and cut the motor. "This thing won't hold out much longer! That guy hit the motor!" he said as the helicopter circled the thin crack. He got off and opened the hood. "Aha! Look at this tube! That's what was making it smoke! And here I was thinking it was some serious damage!" he laughed as he disconnected a hollow rubber tube that was connected to the exhaust pipe. Jake took out a roll of electrical tape, and soon the engine was purring like a kitty after having its back rubbed. "Let's get moving!" he yelled as a rocket raced down at them and after wedging itself in a snow bank not far from the exploded, sending a blizzard of snow to fly at them. A moment later four snowmobiles shot out of the crevice and roared into the thick woods ahead. The helicopter circled the thin crack. Suddenly five figures in parachutes leaped out of the helicopter and landed in front of them! "You are on Mongolian land, and therefore are arrested for trespassing on Mongolian property!" shouted the leader, pulling out an Uzi submachine gun.

Dave veered away as bullets peppered the snow beside him. As the man with the UZI started to shoot at Sally's snowmobile Dave turned around and after yanking the ammunition belt and the gun from the man he whacked him on the head and plowed into the four other men. Then herushed downhill and shot over a small creek that ended in a frozen river. Soon four small dots were seen on the wide, frozen strip of water as rockets and bullets turned the icy lake into a giant slushy.

As Dave sped along on the slippery ice, he saw a rocket fly overhead and explode right in front of him, transforming a huge chunk of ice into a ramp. He shot onto it and sailed over the open stretch of water, barely managing to land on the other side. Jake and Sally also made it, but Chang was too late. The ice cracked, and he skidded to a stop on a big piece of ice floating in the middle of the river. He froze as the ice creaked and slowly started to move down the sluggish river. As he reached a jumble of other ice floes, he slowly started to maneuver his piece of ice toward shore. Then he saw Dave carefully point the Uzi at the helicopter and fire. The bullet penetrated a small crack in the amour and buried itself into the gas tank. The giant whirlybird burst into flame. As it plummeted toward the river, four parachutes blossomed high in the air and started to float toward the icy river.

When the helicopter crashed into the river, it sent a huge wave that carried Chang's ice floe toward the shore. Soon Chang was once again driving on firm ground. He shivered as the smoke stopped coming up from the river's surface and watched the four remaining paratroopers land on an ice floe and shake their fists at him as they floated past. Chang hurried after his friends, who, after seeing him safely land, shot up into the mountains again. Soon Chang had caught up with them, and the four friends raced through the thick woods. As they reached a clearing, Jake's snowmobile sputtered and stopped. Jake sighed and checked the fuel gauge. Empty! He got off and refilled the tank. The three others filled theirs too. "We'll have to be careful now! There aren't any gas stations around here, you know!" joked Sally. The boys laughed halfheartedly. The four teens leaped onto the snowmobiles and roared deeper into the mountains.

As they reached the top of a tall mountain, they looked down and saw a breathtaking sight. They were on the top of a long range of mountains stretching out over the Chinese—Mongolian territory. In the distance was the Great Wall of China. Helicopters circled the wall above the heavily guarded crossing point, and they could see puffs of smoke as the men practiced shooting anti-aircraft missiles.

"Whoa! Those are some big fireworks!" said Jake as the missiles exploded and another barrage was sent up. Chang was still looking in awe at the explosions while the others tried, and failed, to start their snowmobiles. Dave frowned and looked at the gas gauge. Then he groaned.

"These things are empty, and we don't have any more fuel!" he said as the other snowmobiles coughed and sputtered. Jake sighed and looked at his own immobile machine. Then he slowly rolled it under a tree. Then he removed his supplies and the snowboard and covered it with tarp.

"Let's go, guys! If we stay here we'll freeze. And it looks as if there's a blizzard brewing," he said. He helped push Sally's snowmobile under another tree. As soon as the four snowmobiles were all safe and tucked away, the four teens strapped on their boards—in Sally's case, skis. Chang was the first to try the slope. He pushed off and was soon a mere dot in the flying snow. Then Sally flew down the mountain, with Jake's snowboard right behind her. Dave took it nice and easy. He put up the sail, checked it for holes, and then strapped his packs on the back. Then he grasped the horizontal bar and shot away, with the wind pushing him faster and faster. He flew down the slope and soon caught up with his friends, who were trudging up the snow-laden slope. With the wind pushing him, he made it halfway up and then lowered the sail. The snow surfer coasted to a stop. Dave stowed it to the side of a pile of logs and with the help of his ax, made a little hut, with a warm fire glowing merrily in the middle. Dave put on some hot cocoa and some beef. Then he went outside and chopped up some firewood. Then he laid out a wooden floor in the hut and covered it with his bearskin. Then he made a good passageway from the door to a large tree and made a door there. He chopped more firewood and then had a snack while he waited for his friends.

It was late when they arrived, and the wind was howling. The blizzard blew at hurricane force, covering everything with snow. Dave peeked out as three half-frozen figures staggered up. Dave guided them into the hut and helped them take off their snowsuits. Soon Sally, Jake, and Chang were lying in their sleeping bags enjoying hot cocoa and steaks. "Hmm . . . It's pretty good, but it could use a little sauce!" commented Dave while his friends wolfed down all the food. Then he cleaned up as his friends snuggled into the warm blankets. Dave smiled and took out his knife. He whittled a horse and tried to carve out details.

Dave finished carving and quietly put his knife away. His friends were sleeping, and it was time he also laid down! He yawned and put some more wood into the fire. Then he leaped into his sleeping bag and closed his eyes. The next morning Dave woke up to the smell of frying bacon. He yawned and rubbed his eyes. Sally was at the little fire with Jake and Chang, making coffee, sandwiches, and bacon. Dave grinned and sat down on a log. "Boy! You guys sure can cook!" he said as he wolfed down a slice of bacon. Chang grinned, but Jake looked worried. "Hey! Why the long face, bud?" asked Dave.

Jake sighed and pointed to the door. Dave crawled into the cold tunnel and shivered. He opened the outside door and jumped back as a pile of snow dropped in.

"Yep! It's over five feet and still snowing a blizzard!" said Jake as he joined the openmouthed Dave. They crawled back to the hut and sat down. Chang was carving a horse, and Sally was reading a book. Jake sighed and started to fiddle around with a piece of wood. He noticed that one side looked like a crown. He grinned and started to carve. Soon he had a crown with an extra stub underneath. He was about to carve the stub off when he had an even better idea. "Hey, Chang! Let's make a chess set!" he exclaimed. Chang looked puzzled, so Jake explained how to play chess. Finally Chang got a faint idea of what a chess board looked like, and soon they had carved two knights and two rooks. Jake carved out a bishop. Soon they had all the pieces, half brown and the other half painted red. But they had one more problem—no chessboard. So they cut a thin slice from a piece of a tree trunk outside and then shaved the edges off until it took a square shape. Then they marked off the squares and carved thin lines in between them. They dyed half of the squares red and left half clear. The board was finished.

Soon Jake and Dave had played a match, and Chang was slowly learning by watching the moves they made. In a little while it was noon, and the boys were hungry. Sally fried some dry pancakes and some frozen sauce. They finished off with homemade tea. Then they put on their snow clothes and stumbled outside. "Good grief! I'd forgotten how cold it is outside!" said Jake, his teeth chattering. Dave nodded as he kicked at the snow. Chang looked around at the falling snowflakes and sighed. "They're so beautiful!" he said.

"Yeah! And cold too!" muttered Jake.

Sally smiled and said, "Perfect snowball-throwing weather!" Jake whirled around but he was too late. The snowball hit his forehead. Jake yelled and hurled one back at Sally. Soon all four kids were playing around and tossing snowballs at each other. Chang sneaked up the mountain and sent his large snowball rolling down. As it traveled downhill, it grew huge. When it hit Jake and Dave, it sent them flying. Sally was caught unprepared, and the ball bowled her to the side. By now it was as big as a shed! As it kept on going down the huge mountain, it grew to enormous proportions, fifty feet around! It kept going until it hit a small tree. It smashed it down and crashed into a much, much bigger tree, exploding in half. After the cloud of snow settled down, two almost invisible humps were visible in the snow. As Jake looked at the path the giant abominable snowball had made, he stepped back with surprise. The long trail was pure ice! This gave Sally an idea, but she kept quiet, thinking the others would laugh. "If we need it, I will be ready to use it!" she told herself as they went back inside.

Mr. Fung had managed to escape in the confusion following Dave's escape. "Dratted kid!" he thought as he raced through the thick forest. The shouts of the guards grew steadily closer, as their horses pounded tirelessly through the woods. Mr. Fung was desperate. Finally he blew his horn and hoped his guards heard it. Soon a horde of his guards, bearing the mark of the dragon on their robes, burst out of the forest. They saw the pursuing soldiers and, mustering up their bravado, raced among the horsemen.

Mr. Fung, meanwhile, had captured a double edged *suijamu*, which is a long rod with sword blades on the ends. He swung it around, unseating horsemen all around him and jumped onto one of the rider less horses. Then he saw the commander. It was the dreaded Huo the Serpent! Huo had been bitten by a cobra and lived, though he bore the mark on his right cheek. Unusually, the cobra had left three marks instead of two, the middle one the longest. Huo was known for his merciless way of torturing prisoners. First he carved out the eyes and chopped off the ears, fingers, and toes. Then he put the prisoner into a barrel and let water steadily drop into it, until finally, drop by drop, it would cover the prisoner's mouth and then the nose. By that time the prisoner would be only skin and bones and he might have actually welcomed death. But the cruel commander was not finished. When the poor prisoner had half-drown three times, he would be allowed to gorge himself. He was then led into the market square, where he would be flogged harshly on his naked body and have salt rubbed into his wounds. Finally he would be tied onto an iron pole and roasted to death over a white hot fire.

Mr. Fung remembered this rumor as he rushed at the commander, who quickly drew his sword. Mr. Fung yelled and swung his weapon at the richly robed commander, who lightly batted it off. Huo had the best sword in the kingdom. Its blade was made from an unknown metal from a fallen comet. No rock or metal could withstand its crushing blow. Nevertheless, Mr. Fung swung his horse around and swung the double blades at the impenetrable sword, which chopped Fung's blade in half. Quickly he swung the other blade, and that, too, was sliced in half. Just then an enemy arrow found Mr. Fung's stolen horse's chest, and it reared up. Then it gave a last buck and somersaulted over its head. Mr. Fung was flung onto a tree. He barely missed the tree trunk and plunged to the ground. His useless and bladeless weapon toppled to the ground with him as he clutched it by the middle. The bottom buried itself in the ground, and the other end smashed into the commander's back, unseating him and lifting Mr. Fung onto the third-best horse in the province. Mr. Fung threw his sharp dagger at the fallen commander, and after the body stopped twitching, he used the legendary sword to take off the commander's head. He dismounted and took the commander's armor and weapons and leaped onto the horse.

"Retreat!" he yelled. Bringing the great battle horse under control, he galloped out of the forest. His faithful guards left the field of battle and quickly plunged into the open field beyond. After crossing the river Yung and climbing halfway up the mountain beyond, they stopped to rest. The horses were exhausted, and eight of their men were missing. Mr. Fung sighed but then brightened up. "Hey! I have one of the best swords in the whole country. I have the third-best horse in the province, and I have defeated Huo the Serpent! If that isn't an act of bravery, then I don't know what is!" He smiled proudly and yelled at the guards sitting around the huge fire. "My faithful followers! I have defeated Huo the Serpent! I have his sword, Dragonflame, and I have his war steed, Fleetfoot! Now I command you to sing a song of glory about my victory." The burly men looked up and laughed at Fung. Mr. Fung leaped off his log and whacked two on the head. "Fools! I could behead you for that! Now sing!" The frightened guards whispered among themselves and then started rasping out some words that might have resembled a song.

You, the mighty warlord sire!
You defeated the empire!
We forever worship you!
Our lives and souls we pledge too!

Mr. Fung smiled and basked in the glory. Then he ordered some food and soon was up to date with the happenings. "Very well! We will set off across the mountains at once!" The guards groaned. Then Mr. Fung had a better idea. "Very well. We will remain here for the night, but we leave in the morning. Oh, and there better be some breakfast ready as soon as I wake up!" he yelled, and he chuckled as the guards looked around uneasily. It was hard to have breakfast ready at four fifteen sharp! Then he yawned. He knew he'd better go to sleep right away, if he was to be well rested on the morrow. Little did he know that sleep would come in a freaky way. For though the terrors of his capture were gone, the horrors remained in his brain, and in sleep they looked much, much worse.

The next day Jake woke up early. He smiled and got up. After putting more wood onto the coals, he fired up the flames and put a frying pan over the fire. Next he poured some oil into the pan and put four packages of bacon in it. Next he put some bread slices next to the fire to heat up and sat down on little stump. He took out his bow and arrows and looked the arrows over. He sharpened them and waxed the string on the bow. *This is going to be a long day!* he thought, and he picked up his sword. Its old blade glimmered as he pulled it from the sheath. Then he pulled out the new princely sword and studied its blade. It was unmarked, the handle covered with leather. It was light to swing, a much better sword than Jake's old one. Jake sighed and polished it. Then he polished the shield and helmet. The gold-covered armor glistened in the light. Then he took out Sally's suit. It was light blue and almost transparent, like ice. The dagger was curved and very delicate, with a silver handle, embroidered with turquoise stones. The bow was not made of wood but of some rubberlike material. The string was like a fishing line and light blue, like the rest of the bow. The arrows were all made of a light metal and feathered with the feathers of a blue jay. The tips were turquoise also, with a tiny diamond stud on the front of each arrow. Sally's helmet showed a snarling wildcat, also in blue, with the visor inside the wide open mouth. Jake's was a hissing serpent. Chang's armor was red and had a falcon's head on the helmet. He had a suijama too. The armor itself was covered in ruby feathers and had claws sticking out of the fists.

Dave's set was the largest, pure black, with dark purple veins and little wings off the back. His helmet showed a weird monster with glowing eyes. It had two huge pairs of fangs, the smaller pair on the bottom, the bigger pair on the top. The huge broadsword was edged with black diamonds and had carved purple veins. When Dave poured a special substance on it and lit it, it burned with a purple flame for three hours, even underwater. The only thing that could douse it was a real flame.

Jake finished examining the beautiful armor and blades and started to get up. He heard a muffled growl. Jake stood stock still and listened carefully. Yes! There it was again, only louder this time. Jake picked up his old sword and his bow. Then he carefully opened the skin door and sneaked down the passageway. He came to the outside door and quietly opened it. Then he froze. Not ten feet away from him stood a huge grizzly! It was tearing at the side of their hut, evidently after the bacon. Jake carefully fitted an arrow into his bow and whistled. The bear turned around, and then Jake fired. The arrow flew true, and the bear roared in pain, clawing at the arrow in its neck. Before it had time to attack Jake, another arrow pierced its chest. The grizzly's eyes turned red, and he turned wild. He turned on Jake. Giving three loud roars, it raced at Jake. Jake leaped back and sent one more arrow into the bear's eye. The huge grizzly shrieked in pain and stumbled toward Jake. Finally Jake pulled out his sword and walloped off the huge creature's head. The body swayed and then tumbled to the ground. Jake measured it, it was sixteen feet and four inches from tail to nose. Just then Dave came out. He looked at the huge figure stretched out on the snow and whistled.

"What a monster!" he said.

"What is?" asked Sally, sticking her head out.

"A great big grizzly!" yelled Jake.

Chang peered into the grizzly's face. "You actually took his head off?" he commented, in awe.

Jake nodded and said, "I sure did, but it was no piece of cake!"

Chang looked puzzled. "What piece of cake?" he asked.

"It's just an expression, silly!" giggled Sally.

Chang blushed and said, "I knew that!"

Jake shook his head and took his dagger out. "We better skin him before he freezes!" he yelled as he ripped off a claw. Soon he had eight, seven-inch-long claws. "I'm going to make myself a glove with claws sticking out!" he promised. Dave laughed and started to peel off the rug-like fur. In twenty minutes they had the fur in one pile. Sally and Chang rubbed off the meat and blood. They put the meat in another, and Jake and Dave chopped it up and washed it with snow. A little later they smoked some of the meat, but they left the majority outside to freeze. Jake guarded it and worked on his gloves.

Suddenly he heard soft footsteps and carefully looked up. There on the snow was a fox, trying to tug away the biggest piece of eat. Jake pulled back the bow string, and a moment later the fox lay slain on the white snow, its blood dyeing the snow red. Jake looked at its red-orange fur and quickly skinned it. Then he prepared the fur and started to sew some gloves. When he had finished sewing them together, he dipped them into some glue-like latex substance and left them to dry. Then he added the claws and reinforced them with a thin but tough bronze covering. He also made an extra strengthener that went all the way to his elbow. Then Jake took out some boots he had been making and attached one small claw on the back of each of them. Finally he put the remaining fox skin into his backpack. At last he sat down and tried on his new clawed gloves. He shredded one of the pieces of meat and clawed up half of a tree.

Dave came out and tried on the gloves. "Whoa!" he yelled as he cut a small branch into four pieces. Then he had an idea. They worked for a few hours to make a helmet from the bear's head. Jake made a costume out of the skin for himself, and Dave finished some snow pants and a coat.

Then they heard Sally calling. The two boys raced inside to find Sally setting out some slightly burned bacon. "Food!" they both yelled and started to eat.

Chang showed off his new bearskin hat as he finished off his hot cocoa, and Jake modeled his bear head and gloves.

"Hey, Sally! What did you make?" asked Jake.

Sally smiled sadly and said, "I tried to make a coat, but I don't have enough fur."

Jake grinned. "Would this help?" he asked mischievously, holding up the remaining fox skin.

Sally looked surprised. "Jake! You're the best brother in the world!" she yelled as she hugged the beautiful orange fur.

Jake smiled, "I'm not surprised!"

Dave picked up his own bear skin clothes and showed them around. He mentioned, "Jake helped me make them!"

Everyone laughed, and they finished their meal. After their brunch, the four kids played chess and checkers. They spent the evening singing songs and telling jokes, riddles, and stories.

While the atmosphere in the teens' hut was happy, the one in Mr. Fung's group was not. The guards were complaining, the food was bad, the horsed were tired, and Lou was mad. Mr. Fung sighed and shook his head as they descended into a broad valley. They had seen the Great

Wall the other day and were now headed toward it. Then he noticed smoke coming from somewhere halfway up the mountain. "Halt!" he yelled and motioned for a telescope. He looked carefully at the lump in the snow from which the smoke was coming and then at the spot by it. It could only be one thing. "Guards! We head up there!" he yelled. *Those pesky kids can't get away now!* he thought triumphantly. As the guards pushed their horses up the mountain, one of the horses shrieked in pain as its rider poked its side roughly. Sally heard the shriek as she crawled outside.

"Jake!" she yelled.

"What?" he yelled back.

"Someone is coming!" she shouted.

Jake burst out of the hut, his sword and bow ready.

"Who is it?" asked Dave, crawling out too.

Sally pointed at the tiny dots at the bottom of the hill. "It's probably our uncle Lou!" she said as the dots slowly plowed their way up.

By now Chang was outside too. "Hey! That's a lot of people!" he said as the dots spread out.

Sally nodded and explained, "Our uncle has been after us since . . . Oh, let's just say a long time ago!"

Chang whistled. "Why?"

Sally laughed and said, "That's what we've been figuring out!" As the dots moved closer, the teens hid behind a snowdrift. Suddenly about fifty arrows smashed into their hut. Sally quickly ran into a snow cave and rolled out a giant snowball. The boys each made one too. Sally waited until the figures were about eighty yards away and then gave the signal.

Quickly they rolled the four balls to the steep part and released them. As the balls hurtled down, the soldiers tried to get away but the balls came on. Some pieces fell off more and created more snowballs. The huge balls of snow plowed into Mr. Fung's men and carried at least seventy down the mountain. The remaining thirty or so immediately tried to use the path the huge balls had left and immediately slid down.

Another horse slipped and fell down the mountain while the rider pushed on, horseless.

Mr. Fung was furious! He ordered another barrage of arrows to be sent, but only about twenty were fired. He decided to take some drastic measures. "Proceed on foot!" he ordered. The guards leaped off of their horses and roared as they charged forward.

Jake was putting on his Chinese outfit when a sack with a note tied to it fell out of the pocket. The note said,

> My dear explorer,
>
> Of course you have noticed that some may attack you, and the numbers may seem overwhelming, but remember always, you are greater! In this sack is the sand that makes the dragon roar. Tie it to your arrow and shoot it at the enemies. The dragon's wrath will open, and the flames shall come out. You will emerge victorious. But remember, the dragon has only one roar! Now go and destroy your enemies! In your other pocket is the smoke that will shelter you as you run for cover. Farewell and good luck again!
>
> Listen to this chant. It will open my most secret doors, and it shows the power that is even greater than Shari, the mighty dragon lord. Listen and bow your head in reverence!
>
> Mighty Father, Revered Son,
> Spirit third, unite in one!
> All the earthly kings and emp'rors!
> Bow down low before him, gods!
> To the most high King of Glory,
> Hallelujah! Yeshua.
> May he give us, earthly kings,
> Power, wisdom, all is his!

Here I talk of the highest God, above all gods! He alone controls the universe, the stars, the planets, and reigns king above all kings, and lord above all lords. May you follow, respect, revere, and obey him above all the attractions of this world!

Your Imperial Emperor,
Qin Shi Huangdi

"Wow!" exclaimed Jake, holding the powder bag in his hand. "This must talk about God!" He lit the fuse and tossed it at the approaching troops. *Kablam!* A dragon's head appeared in the sparks, and a huge fireball melted a deep hole in the mountain slope. The guards screamed as they fell down, burned by the enormous blast. Jake activated the smoke bomb, and they quickly disappeared in the smoky confusion. Suddenly he smashed into something hard. As he looked up he saw the face of a huge burly guard sneering into his before he blacked out.

龙6 THE TERRA-COTTA WARRIORS

"Oooh! My head!" groaned Jake as he woke up. He sat up in the swaying cabin of an SS470 AKA StormBird Helicopter, a steady whirring sound above him. On his hands and feet were handcuffs. Jake struggled against his bonds but could not budge them. He turned his head and froze. On either side of him burly guards slept, machine guns lying on their laps. At their sides hung big knives. As they snored Jake saw daggers hanging from the belts slung over their shoulders. Jake looked around and saw Dave and Chang hanging on the opposite side, still passed out. Their wrists were red from the pressure.

In the back was Sally, iron bars holding her to the wall. She was awake and noticed Jake. She looked glad and then motioned toward a thin dagger on the floor. She kicked in at Jake, who caught it in his teeth. Jake dropped it into his hands and quietly picked the lock on his feet. Then he managed to get his hands free too. The sound of the cuffs hitting the floor startled one of the guards. As the guard opened his eyes, Jake grabbed the guard's gun and dealt him a hefty blow to the head. The big man went out like a light. Soon Sally was free, and in three more minutes all four kids were out of their bonds and heading toward the cabin, armed. As Jake approached the pilots, he crashed the heavy gun on top of a pilot's head. The second pilot managed to pull out his gun and fire. The bullet hit the glass and shattered it. Sally grabbed the man around the waist and sent the man out the window with a judo flip. With a frightful scream, the man plunged down and disappeared in the mountains.

Jake grabbed control of the helicopter and landed it on a mountain with large cliffs on it. The four teens leaped out and stood on the edge of the cliff. With the wind howling in his ears, Jake slid down a rope to a large ledge. He looked at the face of the wall and stopped. A sign read MOUNT LI. Jake ran to the sign and pushed against the dragon symbol on its side. "Come on, guys! Help me! This thing must open to the terra-cotta tomb!" As Dave, Chang, and Sally helped push, the wall creaked and moved. Soon a small crack appeared. Jake squeezed through and lit a torch. Then he gasped. The walls of the tunnel glowed, and before him was a river of mercury. On it was a gold-covered boat with a dragon's head in front and a large, curling tail in the back. Electricity came out of the open mouth, and blue electric bolts flashed through the river current.

As the rest of the group came in, Jake leaped atop the boat and cut the rope holding it to the dock. All four of them stared at the brightly lit uranium canal walls while the boat picked up speed on the quickly moving current. As they passed through arches, they noticed the murals painted on the walls and the terra-cotta men kneeling on the edges, holding bows and quivers full of arrows. They went faster and faster and suddenly burst out into a sea full of electrified mercury. In the middle of the vast sea was an island full of terra-cotta soldiers in various positions. Further up the walkway was a huge castle shining like the sun, for it was all covered with gold. A beautiful marble horse was in position to be mounted, silver dogs leaped about playfully, a golden stag ran through the bronze trees, and a very lifelike family sat and laughed on a couch in the garden, evidently Qin's wife and children. The whole scene contained an aura of peace, as did the castle itself. Jake, Dave, Chang, and Sally walked silently through the golden garden with its leaves of silver and fruits of ruby, emerald, and amethyst. On a pedestal in the center was a crown with a golden dragon rearing up its head. A shaft of light hit it from above as the sun hit one of the prisms installed in the ceiling, giving the crown a shining look. Jake carefully approached it and read the sign on the pedestal.

You may only get the crown by going through the castle test.

Wow! This is awesome! But what will happen if I try to take the crown now? thought Jake. His arm reached out to grab the beautifully inlaid crown. Suddenly he noticed another golden sign on the side of the first.

Do not leave this place with the crown!
For then the power of the mighty dragon will be unleashed!
Star, lightning, sun.

Jake stopped and looked at the little pictures on the side. 星✧, 照亮✎, 日❉ "

Hmm . . . A star, a dark lightning bolt, and a red sun! In the Holy Book it says that on the last day the sky will turn dark, the stars will fall from heaven, and the sun shall turn red! How could our ancient relative ever accomplish that? he thought. Then he noticed a faded picture on the top.

爆炸 ❋

"An explosion!" he thought. Then he remembered the dragon powder, the mercury river, and the uranium walls of the tunnel. "Oh, no!" he cried.

Sally ran over. "What's wrong?" she asked, perplexed.

"This whole thing is a huge bomb! And the key to destroying it is in that castle!" he cried. All of a sudden the scene didn't seem so peaceful, and the castle turned dark and mysterious.

"Well, let's not just stand there! Time's ticking, and we have to consider that Mr. Fung's coming here to try to steal the crown!" said Dave, who had heard everything. Chang nodded, and slowly they walked up to the porch of the castle. Jake opened the door, and with a creak they entered. The door automatically smashed shut, and a bell tolled seven times. They were in the castle!

Mr. Fung was furious! He and his guards were up on the ledge that proclaimed Mount Li, but they still could not get in. He struck at the dragon sign, and it miraculously swung open. Mr. Fung crowed in laughter and led the charge inside. *Finally the elixir will be mine!* he thought. The guards rushed to the river and stopped, seeing another boat there. This one was inlaid with silver and had a griffin on it. The men quickly boarded it and soon reached a fork in the river. They laughed and prodded the boat to the left. Suddenly they heard a roaring sound. On both sides of the river waterfalls were coming down to the sides. The only safe way was directly in between. Mr. Fung brazenly grabbed the helm and made the pass with only inches to spare. Five minutes later they floated out of the tunnel into the mercury sea. Completely ignoring the castle on the island, they made way toward a shining gold-covered tunnel. "We're gonna be rich!" screamed Mr. Fung in ecstasy, as gold nuggets rained from the ceiling. Rubies, emeralds, garnets, sapphires, tanzanites, and even several diamonds broke loose.

The ship stopped at a silver dock. As the guards got off, Mr. Fung noticed a bridge. They crossed it and entered a land of silver, gold, and gems. In the center was a pool of water with a golden floor. Mr. Fung sighed as they entered this dreamland. Suddenly he felt sleepy. He did not notice the room filling with sleeping gas. He did not notice as the other guards also fell into a deep slumber. They had not seen the inscription on the wall.

> ALL YE WHO COME TO THIS GARDEN TO PLUNDER,
> WILL ALL SLUMBER DEEP IN THE DEPTHS OF DESPAIR.

Unknown to anyone, outside the huge mountain an army was ready to storm in and destroy the intruders. Prince Qui Zhao Lang the Third was ready to attack the main entrance in the base of the mountain.

"Enter the tomb and spare none! Make sure you bring all the riches to me and me alone! Do not allow yourselves to be tempted to keep any for yourselves! Now go!" yelled the general, as the prince dropped his hand and drew out a sword five times too large for him. As soon as the army disappeared inside the mountain, Prince Lang dropped the sword and rubbed his arms.

"Oooh! Of all the swords in my father's kingdom, why did he have to give me this stupid piece of overweight iron? It's incredibly unfair!" he grouched. "I'm supposed to look powerful, not like a little kid with a big stick in his hand! I'm a prince!"

The general tried to calm him, "But your majesty, the blade is topped with diamonds and the holy jade stone!"

"Bah! Holy stone, my foot! No, actually my arm! And besides, why couldn't I use my sword, Yuan? It has a good blade and much better balance!" yelled the young prince.

The general looked around and thrust out the prince's sword. "Here! But don't tell anyone I gave it to you!" he said in a loud stage whisper. The prince smiled craftily and handed the general a sack of coins. Then the two of them entered the mountain, clapping each other on the back.

Back in the castle, Jake was in the lead as they walked down the dimly lit hallway. "Eek!" screamed Sally as she passed a huge golden griffin. The red eyes glared at her as she stepped past it. Suddenly an arrow whizzed near her head and buried itself in one of Jake's shields. Jake had tied one to each shoulder and carried two swords, a long one in his right hand and a shorter one in his left. His bow was at his side and the quiver on his back. Dave carried two broadswords on his back and a big shield with the dragon emblem. He looked very menacing in his armor. Sally looked at her own and sighed. It looked weak and fragile. Even Chang's yellow one looked better. Sally drew her dirk and carefully approached the second griffin. As another arrow flew out, the dirk flashed in the dim light, and the arrow fell to the ground in two halves. Jake drew his sword, as did the others. Jake attacked the third griffin. He shoved his sword inside and heard a click. The arrow flew out anyway and smashed into his armor. Dave had more success. As he lifted his sword, the griffin seemed to glower at the blue flame. Dave slashed at the stone statue, and before the arrow could detach itself it was sliced in half, as was the griffin's head. Jake grabbed a suijamu from the wall and rushed down the hall, taking off the heads from all the griffin statues. As he neared the end, a blast of searing flames almost smothered him. He fell to the floor and crawled away as another blast flew over him.

Dave leaped forward and shoved his sword into the fire. The two different flames met, and both went out with a hiss. Jake got up and tried to clean off his left shield, which was black from the heat it had faced. "Whew! That was close!" he said shakily. Sally groaned and wiped at his shield with a kerchief. The silk burst in flames and soon was only a pile of ashes on the floor.

Chang noticed a revolving door under the dragon. "Hurry up! It's slowing down!" he yelled as the heavy stone door started to stop. Quickly he grabbed Jake's right arm and dragged him through. Dave and Sally squeezed through just as the door closed for the final time. Quickly the four teens stood up in the cramped corridor. High above them was a huge snake head with a long thick tongue extending to the floor. Jake and Sally were the first to venture up the slippery walkway, with Dave and Chang following close behind.

"Hey, Jake! Is that gold?" asked Sally, pointing to a basin into which jewels and gold were falling. Jake's eyes popped open when he saw the seemingly everlasting stream of gold falling from the open dragon mouth, landing in the silver basin high on the wall. Off to the side was another open mouth, this one with a big diamond sitting on a puffy cushion.

"Whoa! That's a big piece of jewelry!" exclaimed Dave as he reached the halfway point. Chang's foot slipped, and he steadied it. As Jake reached the top of the tongue, he stepped into the mouth and saw the name YESHUA carved in the wall. As he kneeled before it in reverence, a huge ax whizzed just above his head. Jake yelled, rolled forward, and executed a flip. He leaped the gap between the head and the other side of the wall. There he was faced with dozens of thin strings.

"Oh, great! Now what do I do?" he asked himself. He experimentally cut one of the strings and wasn't surprised when a thin sword slashed down and buried itself in the wood. As Dave landed on the beam beside him, Jake showed him the blade. "Hey! Where's Sally" asked Jake when Chang also landed beside him.

Chang pointed to the side and said, "She jumped onto a side ledge and should meet us halfway." Jake nodded thoughtfully and danced down the beam, carefully eluding the strings. He had to cut one, and a piece of the beam in front of him broke off and fell down to the dark bottom. Jake listened. When he heard the splash he shuddered. *The mercury river!* he thought as he leaped the scary crack.

They continued on until they met Sally in a circular room with four different passages off to the sides. Sally pointed to the right one and said, "That's how you get to the gold! But be careful. Our ancestors were tricky, if you know what I mean!" She smiled and showed them her left hand, which had a long cut on it. Jake looked at the cut and swore. "The bastard! How dare he make impossible traps! I'll smash his bones!" he yelled and stormed into the passage. An angry Dave and a bemused Chang followed him. As Jake ran, he slashed at the walls. His sword shone in the dark. He cut a line and then cut the ax that came swinging at him. A terra-cotta statue with a mechanical swing was reduced to a pile of rubble. Jake was on the war path! He leaped over a huge hole with barely a glance at the piranha pool at the bottom. Once on the other side he grabbed the huge diamond. When the jaws started to close on his arm, Dave cleaved it from the wall. Then Dave and Chang filled their coats and pockets with jewels and gold. They returned, triumphant, to the chamber. Sally was sleeping when they came in, so Jake wrapped the big diamond in his own gold-embroidered handkerchief and laid it at her head. Then they divided the gold and jewels and lay down for a nap. When Jake woke, Sally and Dave were already eating and talking. Jake sat up and got out some food. "We have to hurry! Mr. Lou might not be very far away!" he said as he tucked away some dry fruit. Then he pulled on his clawed gloves, shook off his royal clothes, and put on a beautiful cape. In his armor and helmet he looked like a real prince, bangs, gold, and all. The others put on their armor and capes, too, and waited for Chang to wake up. Finally the native boy woke up and quickly dressed. He pulled out his suijamu and exclaimed, "I'm ready!" Sally grinned and readied her bow. Quickly, armor clanking, they walked into the center tunnel to meet the new dangers.

Though the prince did not know it, he was less than one thousand feet away from his quarry. "Come on, you old women with fairy tales! There ain't no ghosts in the emperor's tomb! He's dead, and that's final! If there are any ghosts and you don't go in, then you'll be the first to join them!" yelled the scarred top general, his face covered in bandages from the rock Chang had planted into his head and his body was burned from the explosion. He directed the army into the tunnel and made sure they moved swiftly enough. "Hah! Soon we will be with the little toy army this once-great emperor provided himself with!" he laughed. Then he turned and helped the prince and third general into the tunnel.

Not a thousand feet away, Dave and Jake burst out of the tunnel into the first ranks of the terra-cotta army. As Sally and Chang leaped from the tunnel, they heard muffled shouts coming from the other side of the terra-cotta army. Weapons at the ready, they advanced to the center of the front wall, on which a huge, hundred-foot-long dragon was engraved. A little amulet hung from its throat. Jake tried to reach it, but it was twelve feet up.

Suddenly one of the soldiers saw them. With a shout he shot an arrow at the little group. The arrow hit armor, and the teens turned. As the army emerged, it screeched to a stop. Four creatures were standing there, straight from the mythological stories that the soldiers all knew. They screamed as Dave's sword burst in flame and turned back toward the tunnel. As Chang ran at the soldiers, he threw his dragon powder bag at the floor, and it blew up.

In the sleeping chamber where Mr. Fung was, a little sound woke them. The guards leaped up and ran toward the door in the wall. They threw it open and seeing the terra-cotta warriors and the troops fighting there they leaped twenty feet to the ground. There were soldiers everywhere! Afraid of getting hurt, Mr. Fung started to scale the terra-cotta wall o reach a small crevice he thought he saw at the top. Meanwhile down below the burly guards bashed the prince's soldiers around like dodge balls and headed for the little prince's general at the back. They picked him up and heaved him at a pile of terra-cotta while Mr. Fung laughed. A minute later there was nothing there but a pile of rubble. As the guards ran about aimlessly, Mr. Fung climbed higher instead of jumping down. He reached the highest spot and saw a bottle. *The elixir!* he thought with excitement. In a lul in the fighting Sally looked up and saw her uncle reach for something and also began climbing. As Mr. Fung tried to grab the elixir, a rough hand pushed him away. There stood Black Bamboo holding a staff. He swung it, and Mr. Fung went over the ledge. "Spare me! I beg you!" he screamed as he scrabbled with his hands, trying to pull himself up. Black Bamboo laughed and swung his staff down once more, persistent in killing Mr. Fung.

At that moment Sally shot one of her precious arrows. The arrow hit Black Bamboo's back and came out his chest. His mouth opened, and a strangled croak came out as the man fell over the edge. Mr. Fung tried not to look down as the burly general plummeted down. He tried to climb up again but found that his foot was stuck. Then he noticed the bottle of elixir. When Black Bamboo had fallen, his staff had knocked it down. He almost fell as he reached for it, but he tried to reach for it. The elixir rolled toward the edge and stopped there, tipping precariously over the edge. He cried out helplessly as his arms grew tired, but no one heard him. He felt himself weakening. He heard footsteps, and there stood Sally. "H-e-Help!" he whispered, his fingers barely holding on. As his final strength ebbed, the elixir was hit by a slight gust of wind and started to roll over the edge.

For a split second Sally was frozen. Either she could retrieve the elixir and lose her uncle, or she could save Mr. Fung and let the elixir disappear over the edge. Quickly she decided. "I'd rather save my uncle than have all the elixirs in the world!" she shouted as she pulled her uncle up on the ledge. His tired body lay on the ledge, and then Sally heard the bottle shatter on the floor far below.

"I'm sorry . . ." whispered her uncle as he fell asleep. "So sorry . . ." Sally smiled and took out her bow. From up on the ledge she shot at the soldiers and used up all but three of her arrows. Then she covered her uncle with a blanket and looked over the edge. Jake was fighting like a wild cat, his clawed gloves ripping up armor and his sword penetrating flesh. Chang was swinging the suijamu with lightning speed, clearing a path through the thick crowd. His long claws ripped swords and even spears right out of the soldiers' arms, and then he used their weapons against them. Dave was the scariest sight. Using his blazing sword, he whirled around, blocking multiple blows with his huge shield and then using his sword to cleave his way through the huge crowd. Suddenly Jake appeared once more. He was hemmed in by twelve big soldiers who carried axes and javelins in their hands.

As he swung his sword around, Sally noticed one man edging toward Jake's back. As the soldier raised his ax, Sally let one of her three remaining arrows fly. The man screamed as an arrow appeared in his eye. In the turmoil after the soldier's death, Jake leaped over a spear and landed on the biggest thug's shoulders. He cracked him on the head and leaped away as the huge man came crashing down. Mr. Fung's guards were literally ripping the swords out of the soldiers' hands and using them until they broke, after which they'd grab a spear and then an ax and javelin. Sally watched as one of the soldiers killed three of the guards and shot him with another arrow. Only one arrow was left, and Sally sat on the ledge and tried to see what was happening. She started to throw rocks down with some success. Suddenly she felt a prick on her neck, and a deep voice commanded, "Stand up!"

Sally shuddered and slowly stood. "Now turn around!" snarled the voice. Sally turned and gasped. It was the torture guy they had seen in the torture chamber! "What?" The thug smiled evilly. "Thought you could get away?" he asked as he poked her harder with the sword. Quickly Sally whirled around and kicked the sword out of the man's hand. She tried to run but fell down. The prince appeared. He noticed the small figure on the floor and his torture man swinging the sword at her. "No!" he cried as he rushed at them, sword drawn. The huge torture man snarled and swung the sword at the shocked prince. "Traitor!" cried the young prince as the burly soldier stabbed at him. He swung at him and then executed a *roulette,* which sent the guard to the edge of the ledge. Suddenly the big bundle of muscles jumped up and hit Sally's armor. Sally flipped and kicked the man off the ledge. As he clung to a little rock, Sally shot him between the eyes. He fell screaming into the very place his general had met his end. The prince brushed the bangs out of his eyes and sheathed his sword. "Thank you!"

"Oh, it was absolutely nothing!" exclaimed Sally.

Then the prince remembered himself. "Stop! We are now at peace!" he yelled to his army over the din of the fight. The fighting stopped when Uncle Lou also ordered his guards to stop fighting.

Sally smiled and said, "Now we can all enter the great emperor's tomb peacefully!" The prince nodded, his eyes shining. The men watched in reverence as Sally, Jake, Dave, Chang, Uncle Lou, and the prince walked toward the amulet. The prince ordered his soldiers to form a human pyramid so that the six royalties could walk up to the amulet and press it. With a grind, the mouth opened and revealed a small room. On one side was a river of oil and on the other a dark hole. On the river was a boat; Sally and Jake got on first and the rest of their group followed them. The boat sped to a large dock on a bay. They got off and walked to a ladder that was suspended from the cave ceiling. Jake opened the hatch, and they stepped out into the garden in front of the castle. Jake looked back and saw that the hatch was fastened to the crown. If he had grabbed the crown from the outside, a terrible explosion would have taken place. In awe, the prince and Uncle Lou stared at the beautiful castle. "How majestic! Even my father's personal castle is no match for this one!" exclaimed the prince.

Jake picked up the crown and walked into the castle once more. "Let's go! Qin's tomb has to be inside, in a place where we would never think to look!" He pushed the door open once more. This time Jake walked to the center of the room. "If I were Qin, where would I hide my tomb?" he asked himself. Finally he stomped his foot in frustration. "This is impossible!" he growled. "No human being could ever find this tomb!" When his foot hit the floor, it cracked and split in two. Jake fell down and landed in a large chariot. The others had barely made it inside when Jake's foot hit the bar that held the wheels in place. "Aaaah!" they yelled as the chariot plunged down a steep decline.

The hallway lit up. They saw baskets of gold and jewels hanging from the ceiling. Jake swung his sword at one, and they were showered with gold. Sally held out her hand, and a small sapphire landed in it. Then Dave noticed the stone bronze horses in front covered with a thin layer of gold. The feet were on top of cracks in the floor, and he could see the wheels on the bottom. Dave swung his sword at another basket and caught the whole thing. He set in down on the floor and leaned back to enjoy the bumpy ride. Finally the chariot slowed and then stopped in a room that had one door guarded by a terra-cotta soldier. As Jake walked up, the soldiers swung, but Jake ducked and smashed it to bits. Gold came pouring out.

He continued, the rest following close behind. They stepped into a low hallway and crawled into a large room. The small group stood stock still. In the center sat a huge golden dragon. Its mouth opened, and a stream of fire hit just below the ledge. The clawed paw lifted up and automatically swiped at them. They all leaned back. On the floor were mounds of gold and jewels. On the golden coins were the images of Qin on one side and the head of the dragon on the other. Jake looked at the ruby eyes that made the dragon look very life-like and then leaped into the mouth, ducking to the side as the stream of fire blasted out. As soon as the fiery stream passed, he picked up the tongue and slid inside. He entered a room, a large oil painting spanning the entire length of the room. As Jake approached, he read the words in the center.

WELCOME, MY SONS AND DAUGHTERS, TO MY PERSONAL LAIR, WHERE I SHALL RULE FOREVER! HERE IS A PLACE WHERE YOU CAN RELAX AND SEE ME IN MY LIFE-LIKE STATE. TO CONTROL THE DRAGON, GO UP THE STAIRS AT THE HEAD OF THE THRONE ROOM AND ENTER THE HEAD. THERE YOU WILL FIND THE MERCURY-POWERED CONTROLS. BE AT EASE, FOR PAST THIS POINT THERE ARE NO MORE TESTS TO PASS SAVE THE ONES YOU SHALL PROVIDE YOURSELF. THE TRUE EVERLASTING-LIFE ELIXIR IS INSIDE ON A PEDESTAL. YOU MAY NOW ENTER!

Jake ripped through the silk and stepped into a golden room with a beautiful throne, on which sat the emperor's statue. The emperor's body was inside the golden replica. Jake kneeled on one knee and bowed to his ancestor. Then he walked over to the pedestal. He lifted the diamond-encrusted silver cover and gasped, for instead of a liquid or a powder, the elixir was a book! Jake lifted it up and read the cover; *Book of Life*, it said. Inside on pages of pearly silk were golden letters. He read the first line: "In the beginning . . . The great God created the earth." The name *God* was written in a beautiful mix of gold and silver. Jake took the book with great reverence, wrapped it in several layers of cloth, and put it in his bag. He walked to the front of the room, climbed up a short flight of stairs, and stood inside the head of the mighty dragon, looking at his terrified friends through the ruby eyes. He maneuvered the arm so that it gently rested on the ledge. Then he noticed a hole in the panel with the symbol "Khou" for mouth. Jake put his mouth to it and yelled, "Get inside! It's me, Jake!" His friends on the ledge grimaced and plugged their ears. Then they walked up the arm and disappeared inside. Jake laughed and went down to meet them.

When they all reached the control room, Jake got behind the controls and let Dave help him maneuver the huge giant to the left wall. Using flames and brute force, they tore the wall down and found themselves in the middle of the terra-cotta army. They made an opening to the treasure chamber, and Uncle Lou's guards began plundering as the prince's huge army moved into the other chambers to get their pay. Then they had a moment of silence for the dead men and left the bodies in the castle lying on some cushions.

After they cleaned and fixed everything up, they left the mountain. Jake hid the huge dragon in a cave several miles away. The prince said good-bye, and he and his army returned to their old kingdom. Uncle Lou, Jake, Sally, Dave, and Chang headed to the airport. "Farewell, my good friends! The prince has offered me a good position in court, and I can't refuse! I hope to see you again!" said Chang, smiling bravely as he shook hands with them all. Then he turned and galloped off on a horse to catch up with the prince. Jake decided to let Dave come home with them so that their father could figure out what to do with him.

"All aboard flight #172! Flight #172!" crackled the loudspeakers as Jake led the way into the airplane. "Good-bye, China! We hope to see you again!" they shouted as the plane moved down the runway. "Great emperor and relative, we will never forget you!" yelled Jake as the plane took off.

龙EPILOGUE

Ouch! What a bumpy landing! thought Jake as he sleepily opened his eyes. The ground rolled by quickly as the plane slowed down and headed toward the hangar. While the stairs were being attached, Jake saw a familiar old Buick racing toward the plane. "Dad!" he yelled. The tires squealed to a stop, and their father flew out.

After embracing Jake and Sally, he shook hands with Dave. "How do you do, young man? Jake has sent me lots of e-mails about you!" he said as they headed toward the car. During the long trip home, Jake and Sally their dad told the whole story. He laughed and shook his head. "You kids are amazing!" he said at the last intersection.

Jake smiled and said, "Oh, and Dad, I brought you a little souvenir!" He handed his father the old sword and a new one from the tomb with a diamond edge. His father grabbed the sword with both hands and stared at it with eyes as big as saucers. He didn't seem to notice that the car had smashed through the garage and that he had parked the car on top of their lawnmower. "Oh, my . . . this is incredible! Y-You mean you kids weren't kidding? This is from the tomb of the great Qin Shi Huangdi!" He was still talking to himself as they got out of the car and entered the mansion.

Dave was in awe of the huge building. As they entered the rich parlor he stared at the dome on the roof and picked up one of the mint candies. "Wow! You guys are rich!" he exclaimed when they walked up the grand staircase. They entered the kitchen, where one of the maids was preparing a Thai dinner. They ate by candlelight and drank some imported Greek wine.

"Three hundred eighty-six years old!" commented their father as he looked up from the sword and took a sip. "Say, Dave, you seem like a nice guy.. Here we are, all one big family! Say, kids, how would you like to make that permanent? We could adopt Dave!" he said, smiling.

Jake leapt up, upsetting the chair and sending food flying all over the place. "Whoopee!" he screamed in ecstasy.

Sally grinned and pumped her fist in the air. Then she ran over to the telephone and told Uncle Lou the happy news.

"Now I will be his uncle too!" he exclaimed, hugging Cousin Suo.

Suddenly their dad's voice was heard. "Hey! Who ordered three tickets to Cairo, Egypt?" he asked. Jake, Sally, and Dave looked at each other and grinned. "We're off to Egypt, Dad! Do you have any road money?"